Everyone has a secret. . . .

Suzanne—New home, new school, new friends. But will the secrets of her past ruin her chance at popularity?

Nikki—Beautiful, rich, smart—and hiding a terrible betrayal.

Luke—Stealing, cheating, lying. Does this brooding hunk have more problems than even he can handle?

Keith—Football star, major heartthrob, can get a date with any girl he wants. Except the one he truly loves . . .

CLASS SECRETS

Most Likely to Deceive

Jennifer Baker

AN ARCHWAY PAPERBACK
Published by POCKET BOOKS
New York   London   Toronto   Sydney   Tokyo   Singapore

AN ARCHWAY PAPERBACK *Original*

An Archway Paperback published by
POCKET BOOKS, a division of Simon & Schuster Inc.
1230 Avenue af the Americas, New York, NY 10020

Produced by Daniel Weiss Associates, Inc., New York

ISBN: 978-1-4814-2875-0

First Archway Paperback printing October 1995

10 9 8 7 6 5 4 3 2 1

AN ARCHWAY PAPERBACK and colophon are registered trademarks of Simon & Schuster Inc.

Printed in the U.S.A.

IL 7+

One

Those girls with their miniskirts and manicured nails think they're so cool, Suzanne Willis thought as she stopped in the middle of Hillcrest High's thick green lawn. She watched as a group of well-dressed teens huddled together, preparing for what seemed to be a first-day-of-school gossip session. Just wait till they get a look at me. I'll give them something to talk about.

"Hey, check out what's coming our way," a girl dressed in a leather miniskirt said to her friend. They were looking directly at Suzanne. "And what does she think she's wearing?" the miniskirt asked her friend, loud enough for Suzanne to hear.

Suzanne rolled her eyes and tried to ignore the obnoxious girls. This hick town is worse than I'd expected, she thought. Just two weeks before, Suzanne's mother had suddenly announced her

1

plans to open a workout studio in a Connecticut suburb Suzanne had never even heard of. No more working two jobs for Ms. Willis, no more waiting tables during the coffee shop's breakfast shift for Suzanne. Now she was here, and the first day at Hillcrest was worse than she'd imagined—and she hadn't even gotten inside the school yet.

"I don't know," the friend replied. Suzanne knew they were staring at her short denim skirt, white T-shirt, and vest. "But she must be new."

"How can you tell?" the miniskirt asked the friend.

"By her desperate look."

Suzanne felt the anger inside her boiling up. "Hey!" she called after the girls before she thought about what she was doing. "I may be new, but I'm anything but desperate."

The girls turned around. Then the girl in the miniskirt started to laugh. "So why don't you prove it?"

Suzanne's temper was approaching meltdown. She had to do *something* to show those girls. But what?

Just then a devastatingly handsome guy caught her eye. What a hunk, Suzanne couldn't help thinking as she watched him walk toward the large concrete building. He had dark hair, dark eyes, olive skin, and a great body. He looked very much at home. Like a king in his castle.

"She's not going to do anything," Suzanne heard the friend tell the miniskirt. "Let's go."

Suzanne spontaneously grabbed the arm of a skinny boy who was hurrying past her toward the front steps of the school. "Who's that guy over there?" she asked him, pointing to the gorgeous, muscular guy at the foot of the school steps.

The boy looked at her as if she were stupid. "John Badillo."

"John," Suzanne repeated to herself as she released the skinny kid. "Thanks."

Suzanne's heart pounded in her chest. What she was about to do had a huge potential embarrassment factor.

She hurried past the girls. When she was confident she had their attention, Suzanne yelled, "John! Hey, John! Wait up!"

John looked around in what seemed to be confusion for a second. Then, as Suzanne ran toward him, she noticed his smile—bright white, with a dimple appearing in his left cheek—when he caught sight of her.

"Hi," he said slowly. "How are you?" Obviously John thought he'd met her someplace before and was trying to figure out where.

"I'm fine," Suzanne whispered. "If you play along with me for the next minute, I'll make it worth your while."

"Play along?" John asked, confused.

"Listen, do you have a girlfriend?" Suzanne asked urgently.

He shook his head, a sly smile forming on his

3

lips. Suzanne could tell he thought this was getting interesting.

"Kiss me," she whispered.

John raised his eyebrows, then lowered his head and gave Suzanne an extremely welcoming kiss on the lips.

Out of the corner of her eye, Suzanne watched the girls pass. They were far ahead of her now, but they didn't stop watching—not for a second.

"Thanks," Suzanne told John after the girls had finally stumbled in the door. "I really appreciate it."

John laughed. "I can't say I didn't enjoy it," he said in full flirt mode.

Suzanne could feel herself blushing. "Well, thanks."

"How about telling me what's going on?"

"I wanted to prove—um, a point," Suzanne said.

"To me?" John asked, his voice smooth as silk.

"No," Suzanne said. "To some girls."

John looked around. "What girls?"

"They're gone now," Suzanne told him. She was beginning to feel foolish. She had attacked a guy she didn't even know to prove a point to some annoying girls whom she also didn't know. "Listen, I've got to go find my homeroom."

John grabbed her arm. "Not so fast. Aren't you going to tell me your name? After all, you know mine."

"I'm Suzanne Willis. Well, thanks again. I'll see you around." Suzanne needed to get out of there, fast. She suddenly realized what was going on—she'd kissed this guy and now he probably wanted more. Typical.

"Hold on a minute, Suzanne. Tell me, where are you from?" John moved them toward the front steps of the school.

She met his gaze. "How do you know I'm not from Hillcrest?"

"If you were, I would have noticed you a long time ago."

"I'm from New York."

"New York. I should have known. I knew you were different from the girls around here. A big-city woman, huh?"

"I'm not usually like this," Suzanne insisted. "Those girls just made me mad. They were acting so superior."

John looked Suzanne up and down. "Trust me, you're the one who's superior. Come on, I'll walk you to your homeroom," he said as they walked up the stairs and into the large building. The crowd of kids seemed to grow around them.

"I don't think—"

John leaned closer to Suzanne. "I'm going to level with you. I'm a big shot around here. Captain of the football team. Girls wait years for me to glance their way. You shouldn't miss this opportunity."

Suzanne just stared at this gorgeous hunk of a guy. "Okay," she agreed. After all, she owed him. And he *was* hot.

"So, what year are you?" John asked.

"I'm a junior."

5

"Too bad," he said. "We won't have any classes together. I'm a senior."

"Yeah, too bad," Suzanne said softly.

John gave Suzanne a hard look. "Hey, why are you getting quiet on me all of a sudden?" he asked as they started down the busy hallway. "What happened to the girl I just met on the steps? You don't have some kind of split personality, do you?"

"No." But now that Suzanne's anger had passed, those first-day butterflies began fluttering in her stomach again. John and this whole situation were making her nervous.

"Prove it," John challenged.

Suzanne took a deep breath and gathered the last bits of her courage. "Okay, why don't we eat lunch together? That way we can get to know each other better."

John raised his eyebrows, a smile slowly spreading over his face. "Why not? I'm sure my friends would love to meet you."

"Great."

"Let me see your schedule," John said.

Suzanne handed it to him.

"Your last morning class is just down the hall from the lunchroom. I'll pick you up outside. And your homeroom is in that room right across the hall. Well, see you later, Suzanne."

Suzanne watched John walk away. Captain of the football team, huh? There's no way he'll show up at lunchtime.

* * *

6

Luke Martinson crossed the manicured lawn of Hillcrest High, sat on the back steps, and looked around. It was early, and everything was peaceful . . . quiet.

The first day of school was supposed to be a drag, but not for Luke. He'd pretend to be bummed out like everyone else, but the truth was, he was relieved. His long and lonely summer had finally come to an end.

Nikki Stewart, Luke's girlfriend, had gone on several trips with her parents. And Keith Stein, his best friend, had gone to tennis camp and then to Europe with his family. Luke had spent most of the summer alone: playing his guitar, worrying about his mother, or working. He couldn't wait to have all his friends together again.

Luke stood up as Nikki's Jeep pulled into the student parking lot. Bright yellow and bouncy, it was the perfect car for Nikki. The car door flew open, and Nikki jumped down, her long blond hair blowing in the wind.

"Hey, beautiful!" Luke said happily.

"Luke!" Nikki half skipped and half ran toward him, her arms wide and ready for a hug.

As Nikki approached, Luke realized he'd lived in a gray fog during the past two weeks that Nikki was away. He hadn't known what a void Nikki had left in his life until she returned.

Nikki threw her arms around Luke and gave him a tight squeeze. "Ooh, I can't believe you're real! I missed you so much. Hey, have you always

7

been this handsome?" She finished with a kiss.

"Welcome home," Luke said, smiling. Then he kissed her soft lips. And kissed her again. By the time he pulled away, they were floating somewhere near Mars. "What time did you get in last night? I waited until midnight for you to call."

"Our plane got in super late," Nikki told him, her arms around his waist. "When we finally got home, Mom wouldn't let me call. It's a good thing we'd already made plans to meet this morning."

"So how was your trip?"

Nikki shrugged. "Baja California is really pretty. It looks just like a postcard. Gorgeous beaches, incredible sunsets. You know the scene—typical tropical paradise."

"Sounds romantic," Luke said, giving Nikki a kiss on her forehead and taking a step back. He wanted to get a good look at her. He'd missed her beautiful smile and the way it made him feel.

"It was," Nikki agreed. "That's why I spent the entire time thinking about *you*."

"No, really, did you do anything fun?" Luke asked.

"Swam in the ocean," she said. "Napped. Read. Went to a lot of fancy restaurants. Did you miss me?"

Luke nodded. "It felt like you were gone two years instead of two weeks."

"What did you do while I was away?"

"Same old same old."

8

Nikki wrapped her arms around Luke and gave him another squeeze.

"I put in some extra shifts at the Tunesmith," Luke added, referring to the record store where he worked part time. "Oh, and Keith and John and I got together for a jam session." He rolled his eyes. "What a waste of time. Those guys are too wrapped up in football to care about anything else."

"Football's important, too," Nikki said.

Luke laughed. "Sure, a bunch of big guys going ape over a weird-shaped ball is right up there with world peace."

"Some team spirit," Nikki teased. "I guess I can't count on you for dates on football Fridays this year. Don't you want to cheer for Keith and John?"

Luke gave Nikki a quick kiss. "Don't worry. Those guys don't need my help. But if you're going to be there, so will I. You can watch the game—and I'll watch *you.*"

"Hey, man. What's up? Can you believe school's starting already?" Pete Brewer, a running back on the football team, asked Keith.

"I feel like we never left," Keith Stein grumbled. Keith had been coming to football practice every day for weeks. He'd gotten used to the ghostly, deserted feel of the school in summer, and it was strange to have the place suddenly overrun by students. Strange, and not entirely pleasant.

"Stein! Hey, man!"

"Hey!" Keith waved at the guy with thick glasses who called out to him. He recognized him from his geometry class the year before but couldn't remember his name. Keith wondered why the other boy seemed so pleased to see him.

Because everyone likes you and wants to be your friend, Keith answered himself. It was true—he was one of the most popular guys in the junior class. Keith should have felt on top of the world that morning, but he didn't. He felt insecure, like the lonely kid he'd been in elementary school and junior high. Back then Luke Martinson had been his only friend. The other kids hadn't paid attention to Keith unless they were looking for someone to pick on.

All that had changed because Keith had *made* it change. The summer before his freshman year, he'd taken control. He'd started exercising and lifting weighs. That fall he'd made the football team.

Playing football had changed Keith's life. It had instantly made him friends with guys like John Badillo—the type of guy who was born to win. And girls were interested in Keith just because he was on the team. In the past two years, Keith had dated some of the most beautiful girls at school. It was a dream come true.

It's strange, Keith thought. You can work hard, get what you want, and still feel like a loser.

Two

Victoria Hill pushed her Ray-Bans up into her wavy red hair. So what if she'd spent almost an hour that morning coaxing her hair into the perfect tousled look, and her sunglasses were ruining all of her work? She didn't care anymore. The first day of school hadn't even started yet, and she was already bored.

Victoria knew she looked sexy in her new cropped tank top and short skirt. She'd spent at least an hour every day all summer lying in the sun, forcing her milky skin to brown.

Now she was wondering why she'd bothered. She could have worn a smelly sweatshirt and a bag over her head for all it mattered. Every face Victoria saw was familiar—in other words, dull. They belonged to the same kids she'd known and gone to school with for most of her life.

She didn't care about the girls. It was the

guys who were the problem. She wouldn't touch ninety-five percent of the creeps with a ten-foot pole. But that didn't mean the other five percent were good prospects, either. Most of them were already taken. And if they were available, she'd dated them already—such as Keith Stein, whom she'd gone out with for a few weeks the year before, or John Badillo, her first real boyfriend.

John was still a good friend, but the romantic part was over. Or mostly over. Every once in a while they still got together. John might not have been Victoria's Mr. Right, but he did have a gorgeous bod. She figured she'd be seeing an awful lot of him that year—unless he got a serious girlfriend. Now *that* would be a tragedy.

Victoria slung her mostly empty book bag over her shoulder and headed toward the back steps of the school—a favorite hangout for all her friends. As she approached she noticed Nikki and Luke already there and locked in an embrace, as usual.

"Hey," Nikki said.

Luke just nodded, combing his fingers through his brown hair.

"Hey," Victoria replied.

"How was Baja?" Victoria asked Nikki. Nikki and Luke were holding hands now, looking very into each other.

"Oh, uh . . . great but lonely." She let go of Luke's hand. "I missed Luke and you guys so much."

"C'mon, Nikki, we've got to go," Luke said.

12

"Okay. Well, see you at lunch, Victoria. We'll catch up there," Nikki said.

"Later," Luke said, already turned toward the door to the school.

Nikki and Luke disappeared into the building, and Victoria spun around and stuck her tongue out at their backs. Love-blitzed zombies. They were disgusting. Sure, sure, Nikki was Victoria's best friend. But that didn't mean she wasn't hard to take sometimes. Luke and Nikki had been together ever since Nikki was a freshman—two whole years. Hanging on to one guy that long wasn't Victoria's style, but she was still envious. At least Nikki could be sure she'd have someone to hang out with on Saturday nights.

Before jealousy took over, Victoria noticed Ian Houghton a few feet away, his long blond hair in a sexy ponytail. He was sitting on the steps, reading, oblivious to the noise around him. Ian was definitely part of the five percent of interesting guys at Hillcrest. In fact, Victoria would have put him in the top one percent.

What was he doing *reading*, though? It was the first day of school, so he couldn't have been doing homework. Any normal guy would be hanging out with his friends.

Okay, so that was the downside of Ian. But the upside was even more compelling. First of all, he was more than cute. He was tall, with long, muscular legs. His green eyes were accented by impossibly long, impossibly sexy eyelashes. And the biggest plus was that Victoria had never dated him. But then again, neither had anyone else—at least not anyone at Hillcrest.

Ian was so into his books and his computer that he didn't seem to have time for girls. He was in the computer club—Victoria called it the Geek Guild—but he was a total hunk. And she knew getting Ian to tear himself away from his computer long enough to notice her would be the ultimate challenge.

She had to take charge of this situation. Victoria carefully walked the few feet it took to close the gap between them. "Hi," she purred as she stood in front of Ian.

"Hi," Ian mumbled without looking up.

"What are you doing?" Victoria leaned closer, determined to make him take notice.

"Reading."

"Reading what?'

Ian smiled and—finally!—lifted his head to face her. "A book. Why? What do *you* usually read?"

"Palms," Victoria said smoothly. "Want me to read yours?"

"Uh—sure, why not?" Ian held out his hand.

Victoria sat down next to him and gently pulled his hand closer. He even had great hands, with long, tanned fingers. Victoria traced his life line softly. "See this bump right here?"

"I guess so." Ian didn't sound all that interested, but at least he was listening to her.

14

"It means you're going to meet a mysterious woman," Victoria predicted.

"Mysterious?" A loud voice came from above Victoria's head.

Victoria clenched her teeth. She knew who it was without looking. That voice could only belong to big-mouth Sally Ross, Ian's cousin. Victoria couldn't stand Sally—she was obnoxious and wore ugly clothes. Worst of all, she thought she was a stand-up comic.

"Hey, Sally," Ian said.

"Hi, Ian," Sally said, a smile forming on her lips. "I'm happy to hear about your mystery woman. I wonder who it could be. . . . Well, at least you know it isn't Victoria here."

Victoria let go of Ian's hand and stood up to face Sally. "How can you be so sure?" she demanded.

"Easy," Sally said. "You could never be anyone's mystery woman because you're much too obvious."

"What's that supposed to mean?" Victoria asked, trying to prevent herself from losing her temper with Sally. After all, she wanted Ian to find her attractive, and fighting with his cousin definitely wasn't the way to do it.

"Oh, I don't know. . . . Hey, what happened to your shirt?" Sally asked, slowly looking from Victoria's face to her bare stomach. "Did you leave it in the dryer too long?"

Victoria chose to ignore Sally and her unfunny routine rather than play along. She gave Sally a withering look. Then she smiled at Ian. "See you later," she said sweetly. "I hope we have some classes together this year."

"Later," Ian said.

Victoria didn't mind anymore that it was time to begin another school year. She had picked her target and was going to do everything possible to get Ian interested in her. Loudmouth Sally Ross couldn't stop her. And neither could the Geek Guild.

Deb Johnson turned a corner, and Hillcrest High came into view. She started to walk faster, impatient to join the gang sitting on the school's back steps. Deb loved the first day of school. It was a fresh beginning, full of promise, a time when anything could happen.

As Deb waited for the Don't Walk light to change, she crossed her fingers, closed her eyes, and made a familiar wish. This year please let me find the perfect guy and fall in love, Deb silently prayed. It was all she wanted from her junior year.

Deb's sixteenth birthday was only weeks away. Sweet sixteen and never been kissed . . . That might have been fine for movie heroines in the 1950s, but this was the 1990s. Deb wondered for the zillionth time what was wrong with her. Why hadn't she ever been on a date? Why hadn't she ever kissed a boy? It made her feel like a total freak. All of her friends went on plenty of dates. They'd all kissed at least one boy . . . if not more.

But a kiss wasn't what Deb wanted, anyway. She wanted a boyfriend. Someone who would walk down the hall with her, call her on the phone, go out to movies with her. Someone who would tell her he loved her. The right guy existed somewhere—if only Deb could find him.

She crossed the street and hurried toward school. Maybe her special someone was at Hillcrest High. Maybe she'd meet him this year. Maybe, right that minute, he was dreaming about meeting *her*.

Suzanne walked into her last morning class. It had taken her practically forever to find the right room, so she was one of the last people to arrive. Only two seats—both in the front row—were empty. She chose one next to a guy with horn-rimmed glasses and thin blond hair. He gave her a weak smile. Great, just what I need, a front-row seat next to a major brain, she thought, rolling her eyes.

"Is this third-year English?" Suzanne asked.

The nerdy guy raised his eyebrows. "Yeah."

Thrilling conversation. Suzanne smiled at him again. Then she twisted a lock of hair around her finger and inspected it for split ends. Suzanne had tried to be friendly all morning, smiling and starting conversations whenever she had a chance. Most kids had been polite but distant.

17

Suzanne figured they'd all known she was new.

She studied the other kids. They didn't look like the rich brats she'd expected. If anything, their clothes were grungier than what the kids at her old school in Brooklyn wore. But then these kids were beautiful in the way Thoroughbred horses were beautiful. Their skin was clear, their hair was shiny. They looked healthy, well rested, well fed. It was creepy—as if they had somehow figured out a way to avoid zits, hormones, and the other disgusting parts of being a teenager.

Suzanne told herself she didn't belong at Hillcrest High. She wasn't nearly perfect enough. John would blow her off at lunchtime and she'd spend the next two years without exchanging another word with anyone.

Maybe I could move back to Brooklyn and live with Grammy and Pops, Suzanne thought. She and her mother had lived with her grandparents all of her life.

But she knew that moving was not really an option. It was just that feeling like an outsider was a completely new experience for Suzanne— and she didn't like it. But she could change all that. She made a silent pact with herself right there in third-year English: I'm going to do whatever it takes to be popular. And I won't let these stuck-up brats get in my way, either. I'll do anything—and I mean anything—to make sure people know not to mess with Suzanne Willis.

Three

"So, Deb, did you do it this summer?" Victoria asked as she put her lunch tray down on the table and slid into the seat next to Deb Johnson.

Deb's smile faded. She glanced down at her yogurt.

"Don't be such a pig," Nikki told Victoria.

"Sorry, Deb," Victoria said, not sounding the least bit sorry. "It's been a long summer. I forgot how sensitive you are."

"And I forgot how crude *you* are," Deb countered.

Nikki smiled. Deb had a reputation for being sweet and innocent, but Nikki knew Deb could stand up for herself.

"So how about it?" Victoria asked Deb. "Did you have an S.R.?"

"A what?" Deb asked.

"A summer romance," Nikki explained, rolling her eyes at Victoria.

"Um—no, I didn't," Deb said.

"Why not?" Victoria demanded. "Weren't there any cute guys on Martha's Vineyard?"

"Are you kidding?" Deb asked. "The place was swarming with cute guys. Most of them were in college."

"Older men? Excellent!" Victoria sounded jealous. She moved closer to Deb as she asked, "So why didn't you hook up with one of them?"

Deb shrugged. "Sometimes I wonder if there's something wrong with me."

"There isn't," Nikki said quickly.

"There *is*," Victoria said, taking a sip of diet cola from the can on her tray. "You don't try hard enough."

"I do try," Deb said, giving up on her yogurt. "Or at least I try to try."

"While you were on vacation, did you even go to the beach?" Victoria asked.

"Of course!" Deb exclaimed.

"How small was your bathing suit?" Victoria asked.

"That's so gross!" Nikki said.

"Was it at least a bikini?" Victoria insisted.

"Stop it," Nikki ordered Victoria. "You don't have to be sleazy to get a guy."

"Well, a little skin doesn't hurt," Victoria said. "But okay. If Deb wants to dress like a nun, that's her problem. I still think she could try harder."

"How do you know she isn't trying?" Nikki asked.

Victoria smirked. "I'll prove it." She turned to face Deb. "Describe your average evening on Martha's Vineyard."

Deb shrugged. "Average? I don't know. Mostly I hung around the house we rented. I watched some great videos with my brother, Ted, and my parents. Walked the dog. Read."

"You're hopeless," Victoria said, throwing her hands up in frustration. "Have you ever heard the word *nightlife?* How are you going to meet a guy if you're hanging around the house?"

"Don't listen to her," Nikki counseled. "The right guy will come along."

Deb looked glum. "I wish he would hurry."

"Why wait?" Victoria exclaimed. "Go out and get him."

"Shh," Deb said, looking at the front of the lunchroom. "Here come Keith and Luke."

"Maybe we should let them hear," Victoria suggested. "Maybe they can give you some advice from the male perspective."

"No!" Deb whispered frantically. "If you say a word, I'll tell them you dye your hair."

"That's not true," Victoria said.

"I know." Deb's eyes were sparkling. "But they'll believe it."

"Hey, guys!" Nikki called to the boys as they approached the table.

"Hi!" Luke gave Nikki a casual kiss, then slipped into the seat next to her.

Keith pulled up a chair from the next table, sat down, and unwrapped his food.

"Where's your lunch?" Nikki asked Luke.

"Forgot it," Luke said, eyeing hers.

Nikki slid her tray toward him. "Here . . . have mine. It's the special—gray meat loaf and pea mush. I get to keep the soda, though."

"Great," Luke said eagerly. "I'm starving."

"Here comes John," Victoria said, pointing toward the good-looking guy heading their way. "Hey, who is that with him?"

Everyone twisted around in their seats to look.

"I don't know," Keith said, "but I can't wait to find out. She's totally hot."

Deb gave Keith a shove. "Watch out, Keith. Your hormones are reaching toxic level."

"Nothing to worry about," Keith said with a sly smile. "My hormones have been there since I hit puberty in eighth grade."

Suzanne followed John across the lunchroom, feeling like a rock star's groupie. Practically everyone called out to John as they passed.

"Yo, Badillo!"

"Hey, John, who's the chick?"

"Badillo, you're supposed to be in training. Don't forget to save your strength for the field, man."

Suzanne's heart was racing. But she didn't start to feel really sick until she realized John was leading her toward a table right in the center of the room. Suzanne might have been new to Hillcrest High, but she knew the popular crowd when she saw it. Here's my chance to make a good impression, Suzanne told herself.

"Hi, guys," John said when they reached the table.

Suzanne smiled at the other kids. There were two guys—one really cute one with dark hair and brooding eyes, and one with brown curls and a neck that told Suzanne he was a football player. There were also three girls, all gorgeous—a blond, a redhead, and an African-American.

The boys and the African-American girl returned Suzanne's smile. The other two girls exchanged looks. The one with red hair shook her head, apparently disgusted.

"Who's your friend?" the boy with the thick neck asked.

John put his arm around Suzanne's shoulders and pulled her closer. "This is Suzanne, my new girlfriend."

The redhead looked as if she had bitten into a lemon. "Your new *girlfriend?*" she demanded.

"Yes, but don't be jealous," John said in a teasing tone. "You're still my *old* girlfriend. Nobody can take that away from you."

"Pity," the girl replied.

"That's Victoria," John told Suzanne. "She's

going for the Oscar—best actress in a high-school melodrama."

Victoria gave John a look meant to kill. Suzanne almost laughed.

"We saved you a seat, John." The blond gestured toward the one empty seat at the table.

Suzanne's smile froze on her face. She wondered if anyone had ever died of frostbite.

"Thanks, Nikki," John told the blond. He took Suzanne's hand. "Come on. We'll share." He led her toward the empty seat.

Suzanne was considering hopping a freight train when the African-American girl stood up and pulled a chair over from the next table. "Sit here," she told Suzanne. "It's really not safe to get too close to John while he's eating."

"Thanks." Suzanne gave the girl a grateful smile.

"I'm Deborah Johnson, but call me Deb." She winked at Suzanne, and Suzanne was struck again by how pretty she was. Deb's skin was a rich chocolate color, and her hair was straight with wispy bangs she brushed to the side.

"Since John is obviously too rude, I'll do the rest of the introductions," Deb said after they had sat down. "This is Nikki Stewart." Deb indicated the blond.

"Hi," Suzanne said.

Nikki gave Suzanne a long, steady look and a quick hi.

24

"That's Nikki's boyfriend, Luke Martinson," Deb went on, pointing to Luke.

"Hey," the dark-haired hunk said.

Suzanne's heart did a flip-flop. With his incredibly blue eyes and his hair a little messy, a little too long, Luke was much more interesting-looking than the other guys at the table. More handsome, Suzanne thought. Not that John wasn't good-looking. It was just that his was a clean-cut kind of handsomeness. Luke was more like a brooding James Dean.

"You seem to know John," Deb said. "And you already met Victoria. That leaves Keith Stein."

The boy with the thick neck leered at Suzanne. "It's *very* nice to meet you."

"Back off, Keith," John said without looking up from his lunch. "She's mine."

"How long have you guys been going out?" Luke asked.

"Since just before homeroom," John said. "That's when we met."

"What's your girlfriend's name again?" Luke asked.

John looked thoughtful. "To tell you the truth, I can't remember."

Suzanne batted John's arm. "Quit joking! John knows my name is Suzanne. And I'm *not* his girlfriend." Suzanne directed this last comment to Victoria, who merely raised her eyebrows.

John did his best to look crushed. "But you

25

are going to go out with me on Friday night, aren't you?"

Suzanne couldn't believe it. Up until then, she'd wondered if John was somehow making fun of her, inviting her to sit with the most popular crowd, then pretending to forget her name. "I'll have to check my book."

John pouted.

"Oh, never mind," Suzanne said. "I guess I can spare a few hours to spend with you."

John smiled, but Suzanne noticed Victoria looked ready to explode. She told herself to quit being so flirtatious. It wasn't winning her any friends. At least, not any *female* friends.

"So where are you from?" Keith asked Suzanne.

"New York," she replied.

"Where in New York?"

"The city," Suzanne said.

Victoria rolled her eyes. "Why is it that everyone from New York City calls it 'the city'? As if it's the only city in the whole world."

Suzanne got the impression Victoria was pushing for a fight. Well, she'd just have to be disappointed. "That's always bugged me, too," she said mildly. No need to make an enemy on her first day.

"What's it like living in New York?" Deb asked, moving her chair closer to Suzanne's. "Is it glamorous?"

Suzanne thought about waking up before

sunrise to do the breakfast shift at Mona's dingy coffee shop, crowding into Grammy and Pops' little apartment, sitting in classrooms where the ceiling leaked and the paint was peeling. Then she looked at John, Keith, Luke, Nikki, Victoria, and Deb, and quickly decided she couldn't tell them what her life in New York had really been like. They'd never understand what it was like to be poor—well, not exactly *poor*. More like working-class. Besides, that part of her life was over. Why dredge it up now?

"I guess it was pretty cool," Suzanne said.

"I'd love to check out some of the clubs down there," Luke said. "But I'm too young."

Suzanne met his eager gaze. Wow, he was gorgeous. "There are a few places specifically for the underage crowd. But for the most part, you have to be eighteen." She hoped her face didn't give away her thoughts. This guy was totally hot.

"Even if you're performing?" Luke asked.

Suzanne shrugged. "I don't know about that. Why? Are you a musician?"

"I play guitar," Luke said, sitting a bit straighter in his seat at the mention of his music.

"I'd love to hear you sometime," Suzanne said.

"Have you ever seen anyone famous?" Deb asked.

Suzanne nodded, relieved that at least one of the girls was talking to her. "One night I saw Woody Allen and Spike Lee at a Knicks game."

"Wow," Deb said.

"I spent the entire rest of the game searching for Madonna in the floor seats," Suzanne added, smiling.

"That's dumb," John said.

"Why?" Suzanne asked.

"You should have been watching the game," John said, taking a bite of his sandwich.

Suzanne laughed. "That's what Mark said, too."

"Mark?" Deb asked.

"My boyfriend," Suzanne said. "I mean, my ex-boyfriend." She smiled at John, who seemed unconcerned. He was busy concentrating on his food.

"Have you seen anyone else famous?" Deb asked.

Suzanne grinned. "I spoke to Keanu Reeves once."

"You're kidding," Nikki said. "He is so hot! Where did you see him? What did you say?"

"Hey," Luke protested. "Watch out—I'm getting jealous."

"Sorry," Nikki said, giving him a quick kiss on the cheek.

Victoria threw Nikki a dirty look. Nikki's face showed she regretted being so friendly to Suzanne. She went back to looking bored.

"Well?" Deb prodded.

"It happened last year," Suzanne said, focusing on Deb's friendly face. "My friends and I were in SoHo—that's the cool, artsy part of Manhattan. A lot of famous people hang out there."

28

"We've been to New York," Victoria said impatiently. "You don't have to tell us what SoHo is." She turned toward Nikki and shook her head.

"Sorry," Suzanne said, feeling stung. Why did Victoria have to be so nasty?

"Shh," Deb told Victoria. "I want to hear about Keanu."

"Okay," Suzanne agreed. "My friends and I were walking down the street, and one of them lost her mother's earring and got all hysterical. We searched everywhere. And then I spotted it— right next to this man's shoe. I was afraid he was going to step on it, so I yelled, 'Freeze!' Then I looked up and realized it was Keanu's foot! I almost fainted. I actually touched his foot!"

"What did you say then?" Nikki demanded, earning another dirty look from Victoria.

"I tried to say hi," Suzanne said, "but I was so nervous, it came out in a tiny whisper. I don't even know if he heard me."

Keith rolled his eyes and continued eating.

"How exciting," John said in a monotone.

Victoria eyed Suzanne's T-shirt and vest. "Did you get that outfit in SoHo?"

Suzanne felt her face heat up. "No. This outfit is strictly from the mall."

"Yeah," Victoria said. "I could have guessed."

The bell rang.

The group got to their feet and gathered their things. Suzanne hadn't even gotten a chance to eat. But that was okay—she was too busy meet-ing the in crowd to care about food.

Suzanne stood up. As she did, she noticed that Nikki and Luke were holding hands. Hastily she switched her gaze from them to the tabletop.

She wanted to say something more to the other girls, something to make them like her. But before she had a chance to speak, John slung his arm around her shoulder and steered her toward the door. "Come on, girlfriend. I'll help you find your next class."

Luke watched Suzanne and John disappear through the lunchroom door. With surprise, he realized he was smiling. He had a strange feeling in his stomach. Suzanne is amazing! he thought. With those incredibly long legs and silky brown hair, she's totally gorgeous.

"Luke? Earth to Luke," a loud voice inter-rupted his thoughts.

"Huh?"

Victoria was frowning at him. "I asked you twice already. Don't you think Deb was a little too friendly to Suzanne?"

"Not really."

"Oh, great," Victoria said. "Guys are all alike. They like any girl who fools around."

"You just met Suzanne!" Deb exclaimed. "How do you know she fools around?"

"John doesn't get interested in a girl be-cause she's *smart*," Victoria said, walking out of the lunchroom with the rest of her friends.

"You used to go out with John," Deb pointed out as they continued down the hall.

"Yeah," Victoria admitted. "That's why I know him so well."

Luke shook his head. "Listen, I don't know about you guys, but I have a class to go to."

Victoria turned to Nikki and Luke. "I'll meet you guys on the field after school, okay?"

"Yeah," Nikki said. "Save us a place."

"Me, too," Deb put in.

"Get there on time and save your own seats," Victoria growled, and stomped on to her next class before her friends could reply.

Deb shrugged. "See you guys later."

Luke hugged Nikki. "So where's your next class?"

"Just down the hall," Nikki told him. "If you're very good, I'll let you walk me there."

"Oh, I'll be good," Luke promised. He gave Nikki a kiss on the tip of her adorable nose. Suzanne might be pretty, but Nikki was a knock-out. And she was all Luke had ever wanted.

Four

"Victoria! Hey, wait for me!"

"Katia!" Victoria called. "Hi!"

"I've been looking for you all day." Katia was breathless when she caught up with Victoria in the hall between classes. "How's it feel to be a senior? Hey, I love your outfit."

Victoria laughed. Katia always made her feel great. "You don't look so bad yourself. At least, not for a sophomore."

"Gee, thanks," Katia said.

Victoria smiled at Katia, who was better known as Keith's little sister. The two girls had met the year before, while Victoria was dating Keith. Back then, Katia had been a plump freshman with a minor inferiority complex—which was understandable, considering that she was living in the shadow of her popular brother. Victoria had made Katia her pet project. She'd given the younger girl beauty tips, advice on boys—she'd even taken her shopping. Victoria's romance with Keith hadn't lasted, but her friendship with Katia had.

Victoria was proud of how popular and confident Katia had become. With her long, wavy auburn hair and brown eyes, she was one of the prettiest sophomores at Hillcrest. Naturally Victoria took all the credit for the amazing transformation.

"Are you going to watch football practice?" Katia asked.

Victoria sighed, looking bored. "Only because that's the tradition."

"Come on," Katia urged. "It'll be fun."

"Trust me. By the time you're a senior, these things stop being fun."

"So you're too mature to check out the guys?" Katia asked.

"I already know all of those guys," Victoria said, taking a mirror out of her practically empty book bag and checking her makeup.

"Well, I don't," Katia said. "And I'd like to know at least one of them better."

"Which one?"

"It's a surprise. You'll just have to wait and see."

That afternoon the bleachers surrounding the football field quickly filled up with rowdy kids. Watching football practice on the first day of school was a Hillcrest High tradition. Nobody knew for sure where the tradition had come from, but Keith had an idea someone who hated football had thought it up. The first-day crowd was more of a jeering section than a cheering section. It was sort of an anti-team-spirit day—the Hillcrest students gave the players a hard time before the season began. Luke always said it was his favorite day of the football season.

Coach Kostro had divided the team into two scrimmage squads. John and Keith were both wearing green jerseys. Their opponents wore orange.

The coach dismissed the orange team, then pointed a fat finger in Keith's direction. "Stein, you're going to be the green receiver on the first drive."

Keith nodded, but it was pure reflex. He wasn't paying much attention to the coach. His focus was on her—his secret crush.

Without even trying, Keith spotted her in the crowd on the bleachers. But her boyfriend was sitting next to her, as always. The sun was glinting off her golden hair, and she'd taken off her jacket, leaving her shoulders and arms exposed to the sunshine.

"All right," Coach said, interrupting Keith's daydream. "Let's go." He trotted off the field.

The players crouched down for the hand-off.

"Hike!" John yelled, then grabbed the ball and prepared to throw.

Keith started to run into position and then realized he didn't know where he was supposed to go. Still running, he turned around and waved to get John's attention. Maybe his friend could give him a signal.

"Watch it, Stein!" a fellow green warned.

But it was too late. Keith plowed directly into Pete Brewer full force, and the two of them went down.

"What are you doing?" Pete yelled, jumping up off the muddy turf. "I'm on your side!"

From his spot on the ground, Keith saw Michael Dover, an orange, reach up and grab the ball out of the air. Like a shot, Michael was gone. He didn't stop until he reached the end zone.

"Yes!"

"Touchdown!"

Nearby, two players in orange jerseys exchanged high fives.

Keith got to his feet.

Just then a crowd of people in the stands stood up. "Stein, Stein, Stein, Stein," they chanted, faster and faster. "Yoooouuuuuuu stink!"

"Real smooth, Stein," Pete added in a disgusted voice.

John ran over and smacked Keith on the backside. "Nice tackle. Too bad it was someone on our team. Oh, yeah, and you're supposed to be playing *offense.*"

"It's not my fault," Keith snarled, wiping the mud from his legs.

"Really?" John said. "Then whose fault was it?"

"Not mine," Pete said quickly. "*I* was watching where I was running."

Keith made a disgusted gesture toward the stands. "It's theirs. How am I supposed to concentrate with all these people staring at me? Why doesn't the coach tell them to get lost?"

Pete snorted.

John threw his arm around Keith's shoulders. "I don't know how to break this to you, buddy, but football is a spectator sport. Those people out there are the spectators."

"I didn't notice you inviting your new girlfriend to watch this afternoon," Keith said darkly.

"What do you think I am?" John asked. "Stupid?"

At four o'clock in the afternoon, the sidewalks of Hillcrest, Connecticut, were practically empty. Suzanne spotted a couple of younger girls eating ice-cream cones on the bench in front of Town Hall. An older man slowly walked from his car toward the pharmacy. That was it. Not exactly Fifth Avenue at rush hour.

Suzanne walked briskly through the downtown district, over the bridge above the train tracks, past a trendy bar. A few minutes later, she caught a glimpse of Willis Workout.

The low building was right in the middle of a huge parking lot. As Suzanne walked across the parking lot she noticed the red, white, and blue sign that stretched across the front of the building: Willis Workout Coming Soon—Join Us for the Grand Opening! Yearly Memberships Available. Suzanne smiled to herself. Her mother sure knew how to do business.

Suzanne climbed the steps and tried the front door, and was surprised to find it open. Her mother was usually such a safety freak. She'd never left anything unlocked or unguarded for a second in New York. But, of course, Brooklyn was far away now.

"Wow!" Suzanne said as she came through the door.

The place looked spectacular. The reception area and juice bar were completely finished. Beyond the reception area, in the darkened gym, Suzanne could see some weight machines still wrapped in plastic.

Suzanne could hear her mother's voice coming from the office at the end of a dark hall. As Suzanne got closer she noticed that her mother sounded angry. Suzanne's steps slowed.

"Yes, you owe us at least that," her mother was saying. "Frankly, I think you're lucky I'm not asking for more."

Suzanne peeked around the door and saw her mother sitting behind her glass desk, yelling into the phone. She was so wrapped up in her conversation that she didn't even notice Suzanne.

"No!" Suzanne's mother shouted. "No, I believed that once. I'm not going to take the bait a second time."

Suzanne had never seen her mother so angry. Who could be on the phone? Suzanne wondered. It had to be someone important.

At that moment Suzanne's mother looked up and noticed her. "I've got to go," she said briskly into the phone, then hung up without saying good-bye.

"Who was that?" Suzanne asked.

Her mother smiled weakly. "Oh, nobody. Just—the towel service."

The towel service? "You sounded awfully angry."

"Well, they've been giving me a hard time all day," her mother said.

Maybe the stress of starting a new business was getting to her mother. "Are you okay?" Suzanne asked.

"I'm great," she said too quickly as she began organizing a stack of papers on her desk. "Well, maybe I'm a little nervous. I can't believe the grand opening is next week. There's still so much to do."

"Can I help?" Suzanne asked. "You seem a little frazzled. I mean, you were practically jumping down that towel guy's throat."

"Huh? Oh, yeah, I guess I was," her mother said. "It's just that this is so important for us. I want everything to be perfect. You'll have to be patient with me if I'm a bit crazy for the next few days."

Suzanne gave her mother an encouraging

38

smile as she sat down on the black leather couch in the corner of the room. "I have good news, Mom. I have a date for Friday night with the captain of the football team—the quarterback."

Her mother raised her eyebrows. "A date? What about Mark?"

Suzanne was surprised. She'd forgotten that she hadn't told her mother about breaking up with Mark. In fact, she realized, she hadn't told her mother much lately. "Mark is part of my old life, Mom," she said. "John is part of my new life—at least, I hope so."

Her mother gave her a radiant grin. "Oh, honey, does this mean you forgive me for moving us to Hillcrest?"

After considering for a moment, Suzanne nodded. "It's not going to be easy for us to fit in here, but— Well, I guess I'm ready to give it my best shot."

"That's great," her mother said, relaxing in her seat. "I don't know if I could stand having you mad at me any longer."

Suzanne gave her mother a hug. "Me neither."

Five

"That was delicious," Suzanne said to John as they left the Arboretum, one of Hillcrest's fanciest restaurants. They had just finished dinner and were walking out of the back garden, where they'd dined at a table with a heavy white tablecloth and a vase of red roses. The trees all around them were strung with tiny white lights. It was really quite romantic.

"You're welcome," John said.

Suzanne bit her lower lip, feeling terribly rude. John had said "You're welcome" before she'd had a chance to say "Thank you." Should I say it now, or is it too late? she wondered as she slipped her arm through John's and sighed happily. They continued to walk through the restaurant and out toward John's car. "That was the most romantic restaurant I've ever been to," she said.

John shrugged. "Girls always seem to like it."

Girls? She'd thought John was taking her out for a special date. But now it sounded as if he'd brought dozens of girls there. Suzanne had to remind herself that it was none of her business. She and John had known each other for only four days. It was hardly time for her to get possessive.

"What do you want to do now?" she asked when they reached John's car.

"I thought I'd give you a tour of Hillcrest." John unlocked the passenger-side door and held it open while Suzanne climbed in. Then he got behind the wheel.

"A tour sounds fun," Suzanne said, even though she was pretty sure she'd seen all the sights of Hillcrest before. She snuggled back into the car's luxurious leather seat, feeling like a princess.

If she was a princess, Suzanne told herself, John was her prince. He'd made her first week at Hillcrest bearable. They'd eaten lunch together every day, though after the first day they'd avoided John's friends and found a private place.

John started the car and pulled out onto Main Street, while Suzanne looked around her. Even on Friday night, the town of Hillcrest felt sleepy to Suzanne. She missed the energy of New York.

John pointed to a stately brick building with a wide lawn in front. "That's Town Hall."

"Hmm . . ." Suzanne couldn't think of anything to say.

"There's the library," John added. "And that place is called the Organic Grape. All of the earthy-crunchy types from school hang out there. They serve rabbit food."

"My mom will love that place," Suzanne told him. "Her favorite food is bean sprouts."

John shook his head and continued to drive. "I don't know how women can eat that stuff."

Suzanne raised an eyebrow. "Men eat sprouts, too."

"Trust me," John said. "Real men don't eat sprouts."

"What's a *real* man?" Suzanne said in a teasing voice.

John sounded serious when he replied, "I am."

"Because you play football?"

"That's a big part of it," John said.

Suzanne giggled.

"Don't laugh," John said. "It really bugs me when people don't take football seriously."

"Well, it *is* just a game. . . ."

"Some game!" John said. "The Hillcrest team trains five days a week for a month in the summer. Once school starts, we have practice every day after school. And until the season starts, we also have practices on Saturday."

"Wow."

John's voice was rising. "And it's not just standing around. Coach Kostro makes us *work*.

Plus we have to maintain a B average in school. It's a lot of pressure. And this is only high school. It's much harder in college and the pros."

"You want to play for the pros?" Suzanne asked.

"Yeah," John said more calmly. "That's the plan."

Suzanne was relieved to hear him laugh softly. "Hey, I think we missed the tour. We're already out of downtown. We could turn around," she said, turning her head to look out the rear window of the car.

"Nah," John said. "There's something I want to show you up ahead."

"Okay." Suzanne turned to face front again. She didn't really care where they went. She was just happy to be with John even if he was a bit uptight about football.

John drove about a mile, then turned down a dark road.

"Where are you taking me?" Suzanne asked. She was uneasy about the lack of lights ahead of them.

"You'll see."

They passed a sign that read Pequot State Park.

"The park?" Suzanne asked. "Doesn't it close at dark?"

"Yeah. That's why it's so nice this time of day. All the old people and little kids have gone home." John turned off the park's main road and drove down an even smaller, darker road.

Suzanne wrapped her arms around herself and checked her seat belt. She didn't know it could get this dark—it never did in Brooklyn. It

43

was making her nervous. "This looks like a good place to film a horror movie," she commented.

John laughed. "Don't worry, I'll protect you." He pulled off the road. "This is a scenic overlook. You can get a great view of the lake from here."

"Cool." Suzanne forced herself to sound enthusiastic. The dark shadows from the branches on the trees were giving her a major case of the creeps.

John turned off the engine and the car lights. As the darkness closed in around Suzanne, she felt John slip one arm around her shoulders and rub her leg with his other hand.

Every muscle in Suzanne's body was tense. The more she thought about it, the more certain she was that being in the park at that hour was not a smart idea. There were probably dozens of muggers hiding in the bushes. If John really wanted her to see the lake, she was willing to take a quick peek—and then demand he take her to a well-lit place. Suzanne cleared her throat. "Don't you want to get out and look at the lake?"

"No," John whispered, his hand moving up and down her leg.

"Why not?" she asked, pulling her leg out of his reach.

"Because I have everything I want right here." John nuzzled her throat with his lips.

Suzanne's mind was blank for a moment. Then she burst out laughing.

"What's so funny?" John sounded annoyed.

"Are we *parking?*" she asked.

"Yeah, I guess that's what you'd call it."

"I just figured that out! I actually thought we came here to see the lake." A fresh burst of laughter overcame Suzanne. "This is so cool."

Without commenting, John kissed her neck again.

"My friends in the city would never believe this."

John sat back and sighed. "Why not?"

"It's just not the way we do things at home—I mean, in New York. Nobody goes into the park at night there. It's not a smart thing to do."

"So where did you and your boyfriends go, then?"

Suzanne felt herself blushing. John obviously thought she was a lot more experienced than she actually was. Mark had been her first real boyfriend, and they'd never done much more than kiss. "Sometimes things got a little hot and heavy in the movies."

"Hmm," John said. "I wish I had been there." He pressed his mouth against hers—too hard.

"John . . ." Suzanne pushed him back.

"What's wrong now?"

Suzanne was a bit breathless. During the past week she'd spent hours dreaming of John's kisses, but not like this. The way he was all over her wasn't exactly romantic.

"The stick shift is poking me." Suzanne hoped her complaint would bring the make-out session to an end. But John didn't give up that easily.

"No problem," he said, opening his door. "Let's get in the backseat."

Great. Now Suzanne had two choices: tell John he was turning her off big-time or play along. After a moment's consideration, Suzanne opened her door and moved to the backseat. Maybe he just needed to learn to kiss her gently, to control his roving hands. The second Suzanne got into the backseat, John slid over next to her and kissed her hungrily, running his hands through her hair. It was about as romantic as being licked by a dog.

Suzanne pulled back and put one finger on John's lips. "Shh," she whispered softly. She gave him a soft, sweet kiss. And then another that was even softer than the first. John kissed Suzanne gently in return, and she started to relax. But after a moment John's kisses turned hard again. He pressed himself against her and slipped a hand under her shirt.

"John," Suzanne said, squirming away. "Don't."

"Sorry," he whispered. Still kissing her, he moved his hands away. Then a moment later he slid a hand up under her skirt.

"John!"

He sat back. "What's your problem?"

"What's yours?"

"Nothing!"

"Then why are you acting like such an animal?"

"Why are *you* acting like such a tease?"

"A tease? What are you talking about?"

"Listen, *you* came on to *me*," John said. "You kissed me before I even knew your name. Or don't you remember?"

"So?"

"So now I want more," John said.

Suzanne was shaking. "More! Did you think you could just bring me up here and—and—"

"Yes! That's what you wanted me to think."

"No, it's not," Suzanne said with quiet fury. "I think you'd better take me home now."

"Fine!" John slid over, got out of the car, and climbed behind the wheel. "Get in the front," he demanded. "I'm not your chauffeur."

Without looking at John, Suzanne got out of the car, opened the front passenger-side door, sat down, and slammed the door closed as hard as she could.

John revved the engine and backed out of the space with a jerk. As he sped down the dark park road, Suzanne started to cry quietly. She couldn't believe John thought she was a tease. Had he just been nice to her because he'd wanted to fool around?

John drove quickly toward town. When he pulled up in front of Suzanne's house, she yanked open her door and made her way out of the car.

"Wait," John said before she could close the door behind her.

She turned to him. "What?"

"I'm sorry," he said quietly. "I guess I got a

little too worked up. I was just so sure something was going to happen tonight."

"Well, it's not."

"I know," John said. "But I'm not used to hearing no."

"There's a first time for everything."

"Can't you try to see my side?" John asked. "After that kiss on the steps, I thought you were into me. I thought there was more where that came from."

"That was just a stupid prank, John. I would have used any good-looking guy to shut those girls up."

"Does this mean you're never going to talk to me again?"

"I might not." But Suzanne was already halfway to forgiving him. He sounded so sad, so sorry.

"Please give me a second chance," John said.

"I don't know."

"How about going to the Valhalla concert in New Haven next weekend?" John told her.

"I love Valhalla!" The words slipped out before Suzanne could stop them.

"So come with me."

"I don't know."

"Listen," John said. "I was a loser tonight, but I promise to be a complete gentleman next weekend."

Suzanne sighed. She decided John hadn't

done anything *that* awful. He'd stopped when she'd said stop. Besides, he was her only friend in Hillcrest.

"Okay, I'll come."

"Great."

But you'd better keep your paws off me, Suzanne swore to herself, or I'll make you pay. . . .

Six

"Just great," Luke muttered to himself Monday after school when he found that his mother had left their apartment unlocked again.

Luke stepped into the apartment and made a face. He decided it didn't matter if the door was unlocked. There wasn't anything in the apartment worth stealing—and even if there were, it would be hard to find it. The place was more likely to earn health-code violations than attract burglars.

He must have been walking around in a daze recently, since this was the first time he even cared about living in a pigsty. An ashtray had been knocked over in the living room, leaving ashes and cigarette butts ground into the carpet. When Luke entered the kitchen to get a broom, the smell of rotting food hit him, and he almost retched. The counters were covered with dirty dishes. The living room could wait, he decided, and he went to work on the mess in the kitchen first.

The phone rang, interrupting his cleaning frenzy just minutes after he'd begun. Luke was certain it was his mother. In no mood for her lame excuses, Luke grabbed the phone off its hook and demanded, "What?"

"Is this the Martinson residence?" came a polite voice.

Probably a bill collector, Luke thought. "Yes?" He sounded leery even to himself.

"This is Dr. Morris," the deep voice said. "Is Marie Martinson home?"

Dr. Morris. The chiropractor. Luke's mother's boss of the week. There was only one reason why he would be calling in the middle of the day. Luke's mom must have blown off work again.

Luke didn't want to lie for her. If she couldn't pull it together enough to show up for work, she deserved to get fired. But Luke couldn't afford to be spiteful. If his mother lost her job, they wouldn't be able to pay the rent this month.

"Hi, Dr. Morris," Luke said, forcing his voice to sound more friendly. He put down the paper towel he'd been using to clean the kitchen as he continued, "I'm sorry. My mother can't come to the phone. She has a fever, and the doctor said she should rest."

"She really should have called to say she wasn't coming in," Dr. Morris said.

I couldn't agree more, Luke thought. "That was

my fault, sir," he said. "See, Mom asked me to call you this morning, and I totally forgot. I've got so much going on—you know, what with school, my after-school job, and now Mom being sick."

"I understand, son," Dr. Morris said. "Just please tell your mother to call me when she gets home."

"Gets home?" Luke said. "You mean when she wakes up."

"Right," Dr. Morris said. "Tell her to call me. Oh, and remind her that she's already been out sick three days in the past two weeks. I have no option but to dock her pay for the hours she's missed."

"Yes, sir," Luke said softly. "I'll tell her."

"Martinson!" the hall monitor hollered on Tuesday morning. "You're late!"

Luke felt like telling him where to go, but he bit his tongue. He had enough trouble to deal with; he didn't need to get suspended on top of everything else. "Sorry, sir," Luke mumbled.

"Get moving," the monitor barked.

Luke sprinted to his homeroom, slipped inside the door, and quickly sat in his usual seat. His teacher gave him a disgusted look but left it at that. She was reading the day's announcements in a drone—so what else was new? It was all Luke could do to keep himself from falling asleep. He'd been up half the night before waiting for his mother to come home or call. And then he'd gotten up early that morning to badger her until she went to work. They couldn't afford for her to lose this job. Luke was planning to ask for some extra hours at the Tunesmith, but an after-school job didn't pay enough to make ends meet.

When the bell rang, Luke staggered out into the stream of students in the hall. He felt a cool arm slip around his waist and turned to see Nikki smiling up at him.

"Good morning," she chirped.

Luke felt love flow through him. "Hi, gorgeous."

"You look tired," Nikki said, hugging him close to her.

"I am," Luke admitted, giving her a quick kiss on her soft cheek.

"Mmm. That was nice," she said. "So do you have a big test coming up? Is that why you're so wiped out?"

"In the second week of school?" Luke said. "No. It's my mom."

"Oh."

"I've never seen her this bad," Luke said, combing his fingers through his messy hair. "She keeps blowing off work. Her boss called yesterday, and I had to lie to him."

"Try not to worry," Nikki suggested.

"How can I do that?" Luke asked. "Someone has to worry about the rent and the gas and electric. If my mom can't do it, that leaves me."

"I'm going to cheer you up," Nikki announced.

"How?"

Nikki thought for a second. "Let's sneak off school grounds and go out to lunch. I've been craving french fries all morning."

Luke frowned. Did Nikki really think playing hooky would cheer him up? "I don't know," he said.

"My treat," Nikki offered. "I just got my allowance."

"That's not it," Luke said. He hadn't been thinking about the money for lunch, but now that Nikki mentioned it, he knew he couldn't pay. The past weekend Nikki had taken him to the movies. Remembering that just made him feel worse, because he couldn't stand the fact that she always had to pay.

"I guess we shouldn't risk it," Nikki agreed. "But I have another idea. You could come over after school. We'll have a video delivered. Something funny. That should cheer you up."

"It's Tuesday," Luke reminded Nikki. "I've got work after school."

"So skip it," she suggested as they walked down the hall together. "The Tunesmith can survive without you for a day."

She just doesn't get it, Luke thought. The problem wasn't that the Tunesmith couldn't survive without him, but that he couldn't survive without the paycheck. "We'll see," Luke said, even though he knew he couldn't skip work.

"Great," Nikki said. "And don't forget you

have the Valhalla concert to look forward to. That will definitely cheer you up."

"Did you get the tickets yet?"

"I'm going to New Haven tomorrow."

"Nikki," Luke began slowly, "I know you're looking forward to the concert, but there's no way I can go. The tickets cost a fortune."

A look of disappointment passed over Nikki's face. But then she smiled. "I understand."

"Cool," Luke said, surprised Nikki had given in so easily. "Thanks."

He leaned over to give her a quick kiss, but she grabbed the back of his neck and pulled him closer. While they were kissing, Luke felt himself relax, his troubles slowly disappearing. But as soon as Nikki pulled away and ran off to her next class, all of Luke's problems came rushing back.

During lunch that day Nikki glanced across the room to a table where Keith, John, Suzanne, and Ian were sitting. "What's going on over there?"

"I think they're playing cards," Katia said, taking a bite of her apple. "It's my brother's latest thing."

"Suzanne and the guys," Deb noted. "It seems like she's met more boys in a week than I have in my whole life."

"Are you jealous?" Victoria asked, playing with the straw in her can of diet cola.

"If I were interested in any of those guys, I would be," Deb admitted. "But I'm not."

"I see John hasn't gotten tired of her yet," Katia said.

Victoria wrinkled her nose. "Not yet. I give her another week."

"Now you're the one who sounds jealous," Deb said.

Katia was watching Victoria closely. "Do you still have a thing for John?"

"No," Victoria said with a sly smile.

"You're lying," Nikki said.

"No, I'm not."

"Well, something is up," Katia insisted. "You're keeping some kind of secret. What gives?"

Victoria leaned forward. Katia, Deb, and Nikki put their heads near hers. "I have a new crush," Victoria confessed.

"Who?" Nikki asked.

"Ian," Victoria whispered, twirling a few strands of wavy red hair around her fingers.

Nikki sat back and laughed.

"Ian?" Deb asked.

"He's cute," Katia said loyally, wiping the juice from her apple with a paper napkin.

"Yeah," Nikki agreed. "But I don't think he likes girls."

"Nikki!" Deb exclaimed.

"What do you mean?" Katia demanded.

"Just because Ian's never with a girl doesn't mean he's not interested," Victoria said smoothly. "He just hasn't met the right girl yet."

"How do you know?" Nikki asked.

"Because he hasn't met me yet," Victoria said, putting down her soda can.

"Well, there's no way he'll be able to resist you," Katia told Victoria.

"Thanks. It's nice to have someone on my side for once."

Nikki rolled her eyes. "Why waste your time? You'll never get Ian to ask you out."

"You are so wrong," Victoria said.

"How about a bet?" Nikki asked.

"I'm listening," Victoria said.

Nikki considered. "I'll give you a week to get a date with Ian."

"Two weeks," Victoria said.

"You don't sound very confident," Deb said.

"Oh, I am," Victoria told her. "But these things take time."

"Okay, you can have two weeks," Nikki decided.

"What will you give me if I win?" Victoria asked. "That is, other than your undying admiration."

"What do you want?"

Victoria considered. "Your leather jacket. I'd look like a killer biker babe in that."

"No way," Nikki said. "I love that jacket."

"Come on, Nikki," Deb said with a smile. "You started this. Don't back down now."

"Besides," Katia added, "if you're so certain Victoria can't get Ian to go out with her . . ."

"All right," Nikki agreed. "But what do I get if I win?"

"Name it," Victoria said confidently.

Nikki seemed to know exactly what she wanted. "Your cowboy boots."

"Which ones?"

"The red ones."

"But those were custom-made for my feet," Victoria said.

"We wear the same size," Nikki reminded her. "Besides, you won't have to give them up if you win."

"Okay," Victoria agreed.

Nikki leaned forward to shake Victoria's hand. "It's a bet."

"Sucker!" Victoria said, getting to her feet.

"We'll see who's the sucker," Nikki said, grinning.

"Where are you going?" Katia asked Victoria.

"To talk to Ian," Victoria said. "Where else?"

As Victoria crossed the lunchroom she noticed several boys following her with their eyes. She smiled with pleasure, thinking how lucky Ian was she had chosen him. Plenty of guys would have done anything to be in his position.

Victoria came up behind Ian's chair and put her hands lightly on his shoulders. "Hi," she whispered in his ear.

Ian spun around, looking surprised. "Oh—hi."

"Full house!" Keith exclaimed. "I win again."

John and Ian groaned.

"Are you sure you're not cheating?" Suzanne asked Keith in a playful tone. She was leaning over John's shoulder, touching his back.

"He doesn't need to cheat," John put in. "He's lucky."

"Luck has nothing to do with it," Keith said, sliding his winnings from the center of the table into a pile directly in front of him. "It's all skill."

Victoria perched on the side of Ian's chair. He scooted over—way over—to make room for her. Victoria fought a wave of annoyance. Ian acted as if she were the plague. What's his problem? she wondered. Maybe Nikki was right. Maybe he didn't like girls.

"Want to play the next hand?" John asked Victoria.

"Don't," Suzanne warned. "Keith is a card shark."

Victoria was about to tell Suzanne to mind her own business, but she bit her tongue. She'd have to watch herself until Ian was snagged—in case Ian liked Suzanne.

"I don't know how to play poker," Victoria told John.

"Me neither," Suzanne said as she massaged John's shoulders. "At first I wished I could play, but now that I've seen these guys giving all their money to Keith, I'm relieved."

"How interesting," Victoria said, giving Suzanne a sick smile. As if I care about anything you have to say, she thought.

"Dollar ante," Keith said as he started to deal. "Twos are wild."

The boys had just thrown in their money when Mrs. Schwartz, the history teacher, swooped down on them. Victoria quickly stood up.

"Hi, Mrs. Schwartz," Keith said with apparent calm.

The teacher shook her head. "When one of the freshmen came into my room to tell me what was going on in here, I didn't believe it."

"Is there a problem?" John asked.

"I'll say!" Mrs. Schwartz exclaimed. "First of all, there is no card playing at school."

"We didn't know," John said.

"Well, you should have," Mrs. Schwartz said sternly. "It's part of the behavior agreement you signed on the first day of school."

"I didn't read it," Keith told her. "Nobody does."

"Well, you'll have plenty of time to read it in detention this afternoon," Mrs. Schwartz said, looking around at the entire group, including Victoria and Suzanne.

"You can't give us detention," Keith said. "John and I have football practice this afternoon."

Mrs. Schwartz gave him a no-nonsense look. "You should have thought of that before you broke the rules."

Victoria stormed back to the girls' table just as the bell rang.

Nikki didn't even try to hide her smile. "How did it go with Ian? Did you get a date?"

"No," Victoria said, collecting her lunch garbage and throwing it away. "What I got is detention this afternoon. And it's all your fault."

"My fault?" Nikki repeated.

Deb giggled, and Nikki joined in. Victoria came back to the table, grabbed her books, and stomped out of the lunchroom.

Katia caught up with Victoria in the hallway. "Are you mad at me?"

"No," Victoria said. "I'm just mad, period. I have better things to do than sit in detention all afternoon. And I didn't even deserve it. This is all your brother's fault."

"I'm sure," Katia said as they started down the hall. "But cheer up. I think detention could be romantic. You'll get to spend an entire hour with Ian."

"Right." Victoria stopped walking. "Locked up in a room where we're not allowed to talk."

Katia wiggled her eyebrows. "Talking isn't the only way to communicate."

Victoria had to laugh. "You are *evil.*"

Katia grinned. "You taught me everything I know."

When Keith got to the detention room, John was sitting next to Ian. Keith knew John was mad at him, so he slipped into the seat on Ian's other side, far from John's angry glare. He slammed his books down on the desk, sat back, crossed his arms, and waited for the monitor to arrive.

Victoria came in, smiled at Ian, and then gave Keith a dirty look. What did I do to her? Keith wondered, even though he knew she was mad because they had gotten detention. Keith could definitely relate to that. Victoria took a seat in the back of the room.

A mousy woman dressed all in beige—shoes, skirt, stockings, and shirt—came in. She hovered in the doorway, looking up and down the hall. Suzanne hurried in and sat next to John. The teacher locked the door after her.

"Detention begins now," she announced. "There will be no talking. If you don't have any homework to do, I have some books and newspapers at the desk you may borrow."

Keith raised his hand. "Yo, Teach. I can't stay. I've got football practice."

The teacher consulted her list. "Your name?"

"Keith Stein."

"You're on the list, Keith. That means you're not going anywhere for the next fifty minutes."

"I just told you—I've got practice."

"And I just told you there would be no talking in this room. Now, if you can't obey the rules, I'll have to give you a full week of detention. I'm sure Coach Kostro wouldn't appreciate that."

Keith sat back. For the next exceedingly long and dull fifty minutes, he glared at the teacher. She just sat behind her desk grading papers— probably flunking some poor student, he thought. She didn't seem to notice his murderous look.

62

When detention finally ended, John and Keith were the first ones out the door.

"Coach is going to kill us," John said as they trotted down the hall toward the locker room. "I just hope he lets us play in the first game."

"He'd better," Keith said.

"Man, I don't ever want to see your stupid cards again," John warned.

Keith didn't say anything. Mrs. Schwartz had confiscated his cards at lunch, but he still had the wad of money he'd won in the game. The money made Keith feel terrific—it proved he was a winner. Keith didn't want to have to choose between cards and football, and he told himself he'd never have to. Just because the school had a rule didn't mean he had to obey it.

When the phone rang the following night, Luke grabbed it, hoping it was his mother. It was well past dinnertime, and he had no idea where she was.

"Hi!" It was Nikki.

"Hi," Luke said, sitting down on the couch in his living room.

"I have good news," Nikki said.

"I could use some."

"Guess where I went today?" Nikki asked.

"Um—shopping?"

"Sort of. I'll give you a hint. I went to New Haven."

"New Haven? Why?"

"To get us tickets to Valhalla."

"Nikki, I thought I told you I couldn't go."

"Wrong," Nikki said. "You told me you couldn't afford the tickets. But you don't have to—"

"Nikki, I don't want to go," Luke interrupted. He stood up and began pacing the cluttered room.

"Come on, don't lie to me. You love Valhalla."

Luke *didn't* want to go. He knew the concert would just remind him that he couldn't pay his own way. He'd probably spend the whole time wondering how he was going to pay the phone bill. But he didn't know how to tell Nikki that. "Okay," he finally said. "I'll go."

"Great," Nikki said. "It's going to be a blast."

Seven

"Suzanne, your friends are here!"

Suzanne grabbed her jacket and purse off the bed, then ran down the stairs. "You mean John is here, right?" she asked, struggling into her jacket.

Her mother shrugged. "All I know is that a yellow Jeep is out front."

Suzanne peeked out the bay window in the living room. "That's not John's car."

"Well, it honked twice."

Opening the door, Suzanne was convinced there had been some mistake. But as she walked out of the house she spotted John in the backseat of the Jeep. Nikki Stewart was at the wheel, and Luke Martinson was sitting next to her. Suzanne hesitated on the porch.

John waved at her. "C'mon, Suzanne, let's hit the road."

Confused, Suzanne slowly walked toward the

car. John hadn't mentioned they were going to the concert with Nikki and Luke. Nikki and her friends had made it clear they didn't want anything to do with Suzanne. On the other hand, Suzanne had to admit she wouldn't mind getting to know Luke better. There was something mysterious about him that intrigued her.

"Hi," Suzanne said tentatively as she climbed into the backseat next to John.

Luke and John returned her greeting, but Nikki gave her a weak smile. This is not a good sign, Suzanne thought. She could feel her excitement about the concert draining away. Was Nikki going to snub her the entire evening?

It's not important, Suzanne told herself. After all, she was on a date with John, not Nikki.

"You look pretty tonight," John whispered to her after giving her a soft kiss on the cheek.

"Thanks." Suzanne relaxed a bit—until they were on the parkway and John scooted forward to talk to Nikki about football.

John was so wrapped up in their conversation, he hardly said another word to Suzanne the entire way to New Haven. Suzanne turned her attention to Luke instead, hoping to start a conversation with him. But he was just staring out the window, looking preoccupied.

Slumping back in her seat, Suzanne's anger multiplied with every mile Nikki drove. If John thought he could make up for acting like a gorilla on their last date by ignoring her on this one, he was dead wrong.

By the time Nikki turned into the overcrowded stadium lot and found a place to park, Suzanne was fuming. Forty minutes in the Jeep and not one word had been said to her—by anyone.

Climbing out of the car, John reached for Suzanne's hand, but she yanked it away.

"What's wrong?" John asked.

"Like you really care," Suzanne whispered, slamming the car door closed behind her. "And I'm tired of being ignored."

John blinked, apparently caught off guard by Suzanne's sudden flash of temper.

Nikki was in high spirits, though, practically skipping toward the stadium. She didn't seem to notice the tension between Suzanne and John as she grabbed Luke's hand and pulled him along. "Aren't you guys coming?" she called back to John and Suzanne.

"Why don't you go ahead?" John called back. "We'll catch up."

Nikki looked puzzled until Luke put his arm around her and steered her toward the stadium entrance. Hundreds of other people, mostly dressed in black concert T-shirts and jeans, were moving in the same direction. Searchlights streaked through the darkening sky, and bursts of feedback screeched from the powerful sound system inside.

Suzanne waited in silence until Nikki and Luke were engulfed by the crowd before she turned her angry gaze on John. "Why didn't you tell me this was going to be a double date?"

John seemed to be fuming. "I didn't think it was important."

Suzanne just shook her head.

John took a deep breath in an apparent attempt to control his temper. "Nikki went to New Haven to get the tickets," he began. "They gave her four together, so even if we didn't drive here with them, we would have ended up sitting with them. So what's the big deal?"

"The big deal is that Nikki hates my guts!" Suzanne exploded. "There's no way you could have missed how mean she and Victoria have been to me every day at school!"

"If you ask me," John said, "there's nothing wrong with Nikki. You're the one who's being unfriendly. You didn't even talk on the way here."

"Because nobody was talking to me!" Suzanne turned her back to him. She couldn't believe he was defending Nikki.

"So we're even," John said, moving in front of Suzanne to face her.

"Hardly!"

"Listen, I'd love to stand out here and fight with you all night, but the concert is about to start. Would it offend you if we went inside?" Without waiting for a reply, John strode off toward the stadium.

Suzanne stood next to the Jeep, still furious, and realized she could either see the concert or miss it. It was as simple as that. Either way, she wasn't getting home for the next three hours, so she might as well enjoy the concert, if nothing else. She ran after John and caught up with him just outside the stadium doors.

As they waited for an usher to take their tickets, Suzanne felt a flicker of regret. Maybe she'd been too hard on John. He obviously hadn't known that coming with Luke and Nikki would upset her. He couldn't help it if Nikki made her feel so insecure.

Inside the stadium, John paused to study his ticket. "Section E—our seats must be this way. Come on."

Suzanne hurried after him. "John, listen," she said to his back.

"I'm sick of listening to you, Suzanne." He stopped walking and turned to face her, holding up the crowd behind them. "You're turning out to be a major drag. I just want you to remember one thing. *I* invited *you* on this date. I paid for your ticket. And that means I'll do whatever I please. Including inviting my friends to come along."

John led Suzanne past refreshment stands, booths selling T-shirts, and an unbelievably long line in front of the women's rest room. The stadium was packed, and everyone seemed to be having a terrific time—except, of course, Suzanne. John finally found the right section and led Suzanne up a steep, sticky stairway to their seats. Nikki and Luke weren't there yet.

Suzanne slipped into her seat and pretended to be interested in the roadies who were moving equipment around on the stage. Next to her, John was as still as a statue and every bit as quiet.

A few minutes passed before Luke and Nikki came up the stairs. "Look," Nikki bubbled as they squeezed past John and Suzanne to their seats. "I got the coolest T-shirt!"

Luke shook his head as he sat next to Suzanne. "It cost twenty-five bucks. It'd better be amazing."

Nikki playfully slapped Luke's shoulder. Then she held the T-shirt up against her chest. "Well, what do you think?"

"It's nice," John said flatly.

Nikki and Luke exchanged glances. Suzanne guessed it was pretty obvious that she and John had had a fight.

After a long, uncomfortable silence, Luke cleared his throat and turned to his right to face Suzanne. "So, Suzanne, you like Valhalla?" he asked.

Suzanne forced a smile, knowing he was trying to lighten the mood. "Yeah. How about you?"

"They're one of my favorite bands," Luke admitted.

Suzanne smiled and nodded. The conversation was pretty idiotic, but at least someone was talking to her.

But then Nikki tapped Luke's left arm. "I'm starving. Let's get something from the snack bar before the concert starts."

Luke stood up. "We'll be right back. Sorry, but we've got to squeeze past you again."

"No problem. Later," John grunted as he stepped into the aisle to let them pass.

Suzanne nodded, quickly sitting again once they had left. "See you."

"Are you going to give me the silent treatment all night?" John demanded after the other couple was out of earshot.

"Probably."

"Well, I don't need you to have a good time," John informed her. Then he leaned forward and started a conversation with three giggly blonds who were sitting in front of them. "Hey, girls, what's up?"

"We're so psyched to see Valhalla. This is totally amazing. . . ."

Suzanne tuned them out as she sat with her arms crossed, completely humiliated.

Nikki and Luke slipped back into their seats just as the houselights went down. There was no opening band scheduled that night—Valhalla didn't need anyone to warm up the crowd for them. The stadium was pitch-black for a moment, and the crowd seemed to hold its breath. Then the stage burst into light and sound, and Valhalla's long-haired lead singer ran out onstage. The rest of the band bolted out after him as the crowd jumped up, screaming and whistling and clapping.

"Are you ready to rock and roll?" Tightly

clutching a microphone, the lead singer threw his fists over his head. The crowd roared its approval.

Nikki handed the box of food, overflowing with what looked like burgers, sodas, and hot dogs, to Luke. Then she climbed up on her seat, letting out a piercing shriek. "Yeah, Valhalla!"

Luke laughed at his rowdy girlfriend. Suzanne found herself smiling, too. Nikki knew how to have a good time, and she didn't let Luke's reserved personality stop her.

As Valhalla ripped into the opening chords of one of their most popular songs, the crowd settled down somewhat. When the flirty blonds in front of them sat down, so did Nikki, Luke, Suzanne, and John.

The first song ended, and Valhalla eased into a ballad. Luke tapped Suzanne on the shoulder. "Hot dog or burger?" he yelled.

"Neither. Thanks anyway!" Suzanne yelled back.

"Go ahead. Nikki bought enough food for the entire row!" He handed Suzanne three burgers and motioned for her to pass a couple on to John. Suzanne took them and avoided speaking to John by dumping two of them in his lap.

Even though she wasn't hungry, she mindlessly unwrapped the third and took a bite of the cold, soggy bun. Yuck! What's wrong with this burger? Suzanne wondered. There was a strange taste in her mouth after that first bite. She realized the burger was almost as bad as her date with John. If she hadn't seen Luke hand it to her,

Suzanne would have thought John was trying to poison her. This was definitely the last time they'd ever go out together. She couldn't imagine what her life at Hillcrest High was going to be like without him—but she just didn't care. She was fed up.

"Want another burger?" Luke yelled after another great song.

Suzanne shook her head firmly. She was still holding half of her first one, with no plans to finish it.

Suddenly Suzanne noticed a huge bump on her hand the size of a quarter. "Oh, no . . ." Running her finger along her arm, she felt a dozen more bumps.

"What was on that burger?" she demanded of Luke.

Without taking his eyes off the stage, he just held out another burger to her. Obviously he hadn't heard her question.

Beginning to feel breathless, Suzanne got up and slid past John, who had the aisle seat. She hurried down the stairs and out into the concession area, where she found the line to the women's room had only grown longer than before. Suzanne pushed through, mumbling, "I just need the mirror."

This is worse than I thought, Suzanne realized as she looked in the mirror. Her face was bumpy beyond belief—covered with hives! Ever since she was a little girl, she'd been violently allergic to mustard. That was what the strange taste was on her burger. Why didn't I check before I took a bite? she berated herself. Could this night possibly get worse?

Suzanne rushed back to her seat, and John gave her a curious look as she slid by him again. She tugged on his arm, only to find an ugly, unresponsive look on his face.

"Help me, John. We have to leave right now!" Suzanne yelled.

"No way!" John yelled. "I'm not going until they've finished."

Suzanne began to panic. It was getting harder and harder for her to breathe as her throat swelled up. Stay calm, stay calm, she repeated in her head. That was her only hope if she wanted to continue breathing. Unfortunately, she was anything but calm. She knew John didn't understand she was in danger, but she was still furious with him.

"Excuse me," Suzanne said, roughly pushing by John one last time. She ran back down the stairs and frantically looked around the concession area. She had to find someone to help her—and fast.

"Suzanne." Suzanne heard a voice call her just as she was about to approach a graying hippie.

She quickly turned around to find Nikki rushing up to her.

"Suzanne, are you okay? Hey, I think you ate something you're allergic to. Your face is covered with hives."

74

"Mustard," Suzanne wheezed, leaning over to catch her breath.

"Can you breathe okay?" Nikki asked.

Suzanne shook her head.

"We need a doctor," Nikki mumbled, quickly glancing around. "Wait right here." She rushed up to the nearest concession stand.

"Hey, there's a line," someone yelled from near the back of the line.

Nikki seemed to ignore the voice as she pushed through the long line toward the front. "This is an emergency!" Suzanne heard her say over and over. A minute later Nikki was back at her side. "Everything is going to be cool. There's a first-aid station nearby. The hot-dog man offered to call for a stretcher, but I think it would be faster if we walked. Can you make it?"

Suzanne nodded and began to cry, relieved someone was finally helping her.

"Excuse us, emergency," Nikki said over and over as she grabbed Suzanne's arm and helped her weave through the crowd. "You're never going to believe this, but I'm allergic to mustard, too, and so is my dad," she said to Suzanne as they continued toward help. "It runs in my family. I've been to the emergency room about three times because of it."

Suzanne smiled weakly. She felt shaky and scared at the way her body was freaking out.

The girls found a door with a red cross on it and hurried inside. Nikki explained to the nurse what had happened.

"Okay, there's no need to panic. You just need a shot of adrenaline," the nurse said calmly as she made her way over to a cabinet on the wall.

Nikki and Suzanne both nodded.

"We've got a problem," the nurse continued, searching frantically through the cabinet, which was filled with all sorts of medicine. "This is hard to believe, but it seems I've run out of adrenaline. But don't worry—the hospital is nearby." She paused to think. "Of course, it's probably not a good idea to send you over there. On a Saturday night you can end up waiting for hours."

"So what are we going to do?" Nikki asked impatiently.

"The doctor is downstairs, waiting for an ambulance. She's with a kid who broke his arm trying to get onstage." The nurse rolled her eyes. "I'll beep her, and she can ask the EMS guys if they have any adrenaline. With any luck you'll be able to get your shot as soon as she comes back," the nurse said as she picked up the phone.

Suzanne sank down into a chair and watched for the next few minutes as Nikki paced the room, running her hands through her shimmering blond hair. Nikki actually looked worried, concerned.

Suddenly a woman in a white lab coat burst through the door. "I've got the adrenaline!" She must be the doctor, Suzanne thought. "Now let's see if we need it." She took a quick look at Suzanne and smiled. "Oh, yeah, we need it. I'm

Dr. Leonard. I'll need you to follow me into the examining room. Then lie down and roll up your sleeve so I can give you that shot."

Suzanne quickly did what the doctor said. Then Dr. Leonard swabbed a spot on Suzanne's arm with alcohol and gave her the shot.

"You should start feeling better in a few minutes," the doctor said, "but I want you to stay a little longer so I can be sure you don't have an adverse reaction to the medicine. Your sister can stay with you."

"She's not my sis—" Suzanne started to say.

"We're friends," Nikki finished, standing next to where Suzanne was resting.

Suzanne shot her a confused look but didn't say anything.

"Well, whoever she is, she can stay," the doctor said. "I'll be back in a few minutes." She pulled a blue curtain around the examining area.

"How are you feeling?" Nikki asked, sitting down in a chair next to Suzanne.

"Better," Suzanne said.

"I can't believe how fast that stuff works."

Suzanne just nodded. Now that the crisis was over, she didn't know how to act around Nikki. "Thanks for helping me," she said shyly. "But I'm fine now. If you want to go back to the concert . . ."

"I'll wait with you."

"Thanks."

Nikki picked up a stethoscope that was lying

77

on the table and started to examine it. "So, how do you like Hillcrest so far?"

"It's okay."

"You and John have gotten awfully close."

Suzanne laughed. "Not really."

"You guys had a fight tonight, huh?"

"Yeah. Have you been friends with John for a long time?"

"I've known him for a long time," Nikki said, "but he's really Luke's friend. Oh, and he used to date Victoria. Of course, most of the guys at school have."

"I believe that," Suzanne said, then quickly regretted it.

"Don't say anything bad about Victoria," Nikki warned. "She's my best friend."

"I don't have anything against her," Suzanne burst out. "She's the one who hates me."

"She doesn't hate you," Nikki said.

"She certainly acts like she does."

Nikki fiddled with the stethoscope some more. "Well, maybe it's because of John. She's very possessive, and she considers him her property."

"If that's all, it's not a problem anymore."

"What do you mean?"

Suzanne sat up. "This is my last date with John."

"How come?"

"Well, as you noticed, we had a fight. And he was really mean to me just now."

"What was the fight about?"

"He didn't tell me this was going to be a double date."

"What's the big deal about that?" Nikki asked, sounding defensive.

Too late, Suzanne realized she'd said too much. She felt her cheeks grow hot.

A look of understanding crossed Nikki's face. "It was because of me, wasn't it?"

Suzanne nodded.

"I—I'm sorry," Nikki said. "I guess we gave you a harder time than I realized."

Before Suzanne could think of how to reply, the doctor poked her head through the curtain and smiled at Suzanne. "Hey, I do good work! You look much better. How are you feeling?"

"Fine," Suzanne told her.

"Okay, then, get back to the concert," the doctor said cheerfully. "I wouldn't want you to miss the whole thing."

"Thanks," Nikki said.

Suzanne and Nikki grew quiet as they walked through the concession area and up to their seats.

"Hey, it's about time you guys came back," Luke screamed over the music. He seemed happy to see them. He stood up and pulled Nikki toward him.

"Yeah, where have you been?" John yelled.

"We'll tell you later!" Nikki hollered as she slid past John and Luke and sat in her seat.

Valhalla played for another amazing hour.

"That was incredible!" John exclaimed when the lights finally came up.

Luke was holding Nikki's hand. "So what happened to you guys?"

"You missed half of the concert," John added.

The four of them moved out of the way to let other people out of the row. In the sudden light, the damage a few thousand rock fans caused was evident. Suzanne looked around the stadium aisles. They were filled with garbage, and a seat a few rows down was broken.

Nikki looked at Suzanne, waiting for her to explain.

"I was sick," Suzanne said, getting ready to leave. "I'm severely allergic to mustard."

"The burger," Luke said, clapping his hand to his head as if he'd just solved a mystery.

"Yeah, but don't feel bad," Suzanne told him. "You didn't know. I should have checked."

They slowly made their way down the steps. When they got to the bottom, John took Suzanne's arm. "You asked me for help before, didn't you?"

"Yes," Suzanne said, pulling free from his grasp and walking ahead of him.

"You must think I'm a real jerk," John said to her back.

"Let's talk about this later. In private."

"No," John said. "Let's talk about it now." He stopped walking, and Suzanne stopped, too. Hundreds of exhilarated Valhalla fans swarmed past them.

"Why don't you stop being a jerk, John?" Nikki said, catching up to them. "Let's go."

"I'm trying to apologize," John yelled. "What's so jerky about that?"

"It's too late," Suzanne told him quietly. She continued ahead, alone.

John gave her a furious look, then moved toward the exit. Luke hurried after him.

Nikki fell into step next to Suzanne. "Are you okay?" she asked.

"Yeah. But I can't wait for this night to be over."

"I don't blame you," Nikki said.

When the girls got back to the Jeep, they found a bemused Luke and a sullen John waiting for them.

Nikki unlocked the car. "You guys sit in back," she said lightly to the boys.

"But I'm the biggest person here," John complained. "My legs were cramped the entire ride."

Nikki shrugged. "So cross your legs," she said as everyone climbed in.

"Wasn't the lead singer great, Suzanne?" Nikki asked as she turned the car out of the jam-packed lot. "I think he's so hot."

"Once I felt better, I really got into it," Suzanne said, thankful someone was talking to her.

By the time Nikki pulled up in front of Suzanne's house, Suzanne's spirits had lifted somewhat. As she unlocked her front door Suzanne had to admit John had been right about one thing: Nikki could be pretty cool.

81

Eight

"Wake up," Suzanne's mother said in a gentle voice early the next morning. "Come on, rise and shine."

Suzanne opened her eyes and caught a glimpse of her mother's smiling face. She started to smile back until she remembered her date with John the night before, and she groaned instead. What a nightmare! She had been so upset when she'd gotten home, it had taken her hours to fall asleep.

"I've got something to show you," her mother said, excited.

"Show me later." Suzanne rolled over to face the wall and pulled her pillow over her head.

"Can't," her mother said, yanking off the pillow. "I'm going to the studio later."

"Show me when you get home, then," Suzanne grumbled.

"I can't wait that long," her mother said, leaving Suzanne's room and running down the steps.

Suzanne was getting interested in spite of herself. "What is it?"

"Come downstairs and see," her mother replied from the bottom of the steps.

Still wearing her nightgown, Suzanne walked downstairs. The front door was open, and her mother was sitting on the porch with a cup of coffee. Suzanne peeked out the door and caught sight of a shiny red mountain bike parked in the driveway.

"I couldn't afford to get you a car," Ms. Willis explained, "but I thought you'd appreciate some wheels. Around here nobody walks."

"Oh, Mom! Thanks!" Suzanne came outside and ran her fingers across the shiny red bike.

"Are you going for a ride?" her mother asked as the two of them walked back into the house.

"As soon as I can get dressed and eat," Suzanne said. "I'll go explore Pequot State Park."

"Do you know how to get there?" her mother asked, closing the front door behind them.

"Sure. I—um, a guy from school told me about it." That wasn't exactly a lie. She'd just left out a few details—like the fact that the guy was John and he'd actually shown her how to get to the park *in the dark*.

"Are you getting excited about your big grand opening?" Suzanne asked as she entered the kitchen. She popped a couple of slices of bread into the toaster. "It's only a week away."

"Well, I would be excited if there weren't still so

much work to do," her mother replied wistfully, organizing a bunch of papers on the kitchen table.

"Why don't I come by this afternoon and help?" Suzanne offered.

Ms. Willis looked up. "That would be great," she said. She finished packing up her papers and left for the studio.

Minutes later Suzanne hurried up to her room. She changed into shorts and a tank top, slathered on some sunscreen, and headed outside.

This bike was nothing like any she'd ever had. There were so many gears, Suzanne had no idea when to change them. After riding for a while, she found a gear that felt comfortable and ended up leaving the bike in it.

Pequot State Park was much more welcoming in the daylight. Following the sound of gurgling water, Suzanne found a winding road that ran along a stream.

"Suzanne! Hey, Suzanne!"

Suzanne looked up and saw Nikki sitting under a tree next to the stream.

"Hi," Suzanne called, braking to a stop. "What are you doing here?"

"I come here all the time," Nikki said. "This is my special spot. What are *you* doing here?"

"I just got this new bike, and I wanted to try it out."

"It's a beauty," Nikki said.

"Thanks," Suzanne said proudly. "Listen, I want to thank you for last night."

"Oh, forget about it," Nikki said. "It wasn't a big deal."

Suzanne paused, unsure of what to do. "Well, I guess I'll see you at school tomorrow." She wondered if Nikki would treat her as nicely when Victoria was around. Probably not. And now that things were over with John, she wouldn't have anyone to talk to.

"Why don't you sit down for a minute?" Nikki asked.

Suzanne was surprised. "Oh—okay."

After parking her bike, Suzanne joined Nikki under the tree. She felt very uncomfortable and unsure of what to say, so she lay back and looked up at the sky.

"So how are you feeling? After last night, I mean," Nikki asked carefully.

"Well, my hives are totally gone," Suzanne said.

Nikki laughed. "I meant about John."

"Oh," Suzanne said. "Kind of bummed out and kind of relieved."

"Relieved?"

"Yeah," she said, sitting up. "I don't think John and I were meant for each other."

"Why not?" Nikki asked.

"Football!" Suzanne exclaimed. "John has only three interests: playing football, watching football, and talking about football. On our first date he bored me out of my skull. And you know what happened on our second date." Suzanne was aware she was being a bit dramatic—John wasn't *that* bad. But she was so nervous she didn't know what else to say.

"Luke and I are just the opposite," Nikki said. "I love football, and he thinks it's stupid."

"That's funny," Suzanne said. Then there was a long silence. Say something, Suzanne silently ordered Nikki. End this awkward silence. But Nikki didn't seem tuned in to her brain waves.

"So, where's Luke today?" Suzanne finally asked.

"He had to work," Nikki explained.

"Bummer."

Nikki was picking at the grass. "Actually, I don't mind. I think it's good for couples to spend time away from each other. And besides . . ." Nikki's voice trailed off.

Oh, don't stop talking now, Suzanne thought desperately. "Besides what?" she asked gently. Anything to keep the conversation going.

"Nothing," Nikki said quickly.

Suzanne lay back again. Nikki obviously had a secret she didn't want to share. And why should she share her secrets with Suzanne? It wasn't as if they were real friends or anything.

Nikki glanced sideways at Suzanne and sighed. "If I were with Luke all the time, I'd probably get majorly depressed."

"Depressed? How come?"

"He's always so moody," Nikki said. "It's because of his mom. She has all these problems."

"That's too bad," Suzanne said softly.

Nikki nodded. "I feel sorry for him, but I wish he could forget about her once in a while. You know, relax and have a good time."

"You're right. People shouldn't dwell on their problems," Suzanne said, thinking more of herself than Luke. "But on the other hand, it's not good to ignore them, either."

"Why not ignore them?" Nikki asked. "Especially if there's absolutely nothing in the world you can do about them."

Suzanne was surprised by Nikki's fierceness. When she turned to face her, she saw tears shining in Nikki's eyes. "I'm sorry," Suzanne muttered. "I didn't mean . . ."

Nikki brushed at her tears. "I'm okay. It's nothing."

"Are you sure?" Suzanne asked.

Nikki took a deep breath. "It's kind of boring, not at all a big deal. It's just that my— I think my parents don't love each other. They fight all the time."

"What do they fight about?"

"Stupid stuff," Nikki said, playing with a leaf she'd picked up from the ground. "Sometimes I wonder if my father's in love with someone else. He gets mad at Mom for no reason at all."

"Do you think they might get divorced?" Suzanne asked.

Nikki shook her head quickly. Now that she had opened up, she seemed eager to talk. "My parents are much too proud to get divorced. They never fight in public. They want everyone to think we're the perfect family—it's such a joke."

"Do you know what I think?" Suzanne asked.

"What?"

"I think you're lucky," Suzanne said. "It's lonely with just me and my mom. I'd do anything for a real family."

"If you had one, your parents would just fight."

"Maybe."

"What happened to your father?" Nikki asked.

"I never knew him," Suzanne said.

"Did he split on you?" Nikki asked.

"No." Suzanne could feel her throat tightening. She hardly ever spoke about her father, and it wasn't easy for her. "He died in a car accident before I was born. That's why my mom is a Ms. instead of a Mrs. He died before they even had the chance to get married."

"That must have been so hard for your mom," Nikki said, tossing the leaf back on the ground.

Suzanne nodded. "I have one picture of them together. It's a faded old photo. The colors are washed out, and it's out of focus, but you can see how in love they were."

"Does your mom ever date?" Nikki asked.

"Tons," Suzanne said. "She's an aerobics instructor, so she's in super shape, and there are always men hanging around. But she never gets serious about any of them. She never seems to like any of the guys she dates."

"I bet it's because she's never found anyone as special as your dad," Nikki said.

"Maybe . . ." Suzanne looked at Nikki with a mischievous grin. "Maybe she'll find Mr. Right here in Hillcrest."

Nikki laughed. "The men in this town had better watch out. The Willis women are on the prowl!"

"Just my mom."

"Come on," Nikki said. "Aren't there any guys at school you like—except for John?"

Suzanne *was* interested in someone, but she'd never admit it to Nikki.

"Well?" Nikki prodded.

Suzanne just laughed. "Nobody special, I guess," she said.

"I'll tell you what," Nikki said. "I'm going to introduce you to all the cutest guys at Hillcrest."

"That sounds great," Suzanne said with a big smile. She was starting to feel more hopeful. Maybe Victoria wasn't going to stop her and Nikki from being friends after all.

"Suzanne!" Victoria screeched at Nikki later that afternoon. "How could you make friends with *her*? You know I can't stand her."

Nikki sat on her bed, untying her sneakers. She glanced up at Victoria, who'd been waiting in front of her house when she'd gotten home from the park. They were supposed to go to the mall. Nikki had told Victoria all about the concert and running into Suzanne at the park. She'd also mentioned that she'd invited

Suzanne to eat lunch with them the next day.

"Well, I like her," Nikki said mildly.

"So send her flowers or a fruit basket," Victoria said. "Anything, just as long as I don't have to hang out with her."

"What's the matter?" Nikki asked. "Afraid of a little competition?" She'd already told Victoria that Suzanne and John's romance was over.

"That's not it," Victoria said darkly. "I just don't trust her."

"What are you talking about?" Nikki asked.

"Listen, I'm only telling you this because I'm your friend," Victoria said. "I don't like the way Suzanne looks at Luke."

Nikki had to laugh at that. "Victoria, get real. You can't even say good morning without flirting."

"With most guys, that's true," Victoria admitted. "But I never, ever flirt with Luke."

Nikki got up and brushed her hair. "Thanks for the warning. But the truth is, I'm not worried. I don't think Suzanne is the boyfriend-stealing type. And I definitely know I can trust Luke. We've been together for two years."

"That's exactly why you should watch out," Victoria insisted as Nikki smoothed on some lipstick. "After all that time, Luke is bound to take you for granted. Now is the perfect time for Suzanne to hit the scene and sweep him off his feet."

Nikki rolled her eyes. "You've been watching too many soap operas."

"Maybe you haven't been watching enough," Victoria countered.

"Come on, let's go." Nikki picked up her purse. "I hope some shopping will cure your paranoia."

"I don't want to be cured," Victoria said.

"But you do want some new clothes," Nikki reminded her. "So let's go."

Nikki wasn't surprised by Victoria's reaction to Nikki's newfound friendship with Suzanne. But she was surprised when she felt a tiny flicker of doubt. She didn't know Suzanne very well. What if she *was* interested in Luke? Nikki tried to push the thought out of her mind, but it wouldn't go away.

"Nikki, please tell me what's going on," Luke begged. It was Thursday afternoon—four days since Nikki had gone to the mall with Victoria. School had just ended, and Luke and Nikki were walking toward the student parking lot.

It had been a crazy week. On Monday all anyone could talk about was the concert and the fact that Suzanne, a newcomer, had dumped John, the popular quarterback. No one could believe it. But Nikki knew that for the most part, the unexpected development had worked in Suzanne's favor. Before, most of the kids had just thought she was hanging on to John to be part of the in crowd. Now almost everyone seemed to agree that Suzanne was a force to be reckoned with.

Suzanne had started eating lunch with Nikki and her friends. And even though she knew she had nothing to worry about, Nikki found herself watching Luke and Suzanne for any signs of attraction between the two. She'd found plenty—Suzanne's laughing at Luke's jokes, Luke's going all dreamy-eyed whenever Suzanne was around. Nikki had begun to suspect that Victoria was right about the two of them, and it made her crazy. Luke had asked her repeatedly what was up, but she continued to lie, telling him it was nothing.

"Let's listen to some music," Nikki suggested as she and Luke climbed into her Jeep.

Luke fastened his seat belt. "My boss just gave me a copy of the new Cypress CD. Some crazy lady insisted on returning it, even though it was opened and she'd bought it weeks ago. It's in my backpack. Want to hear it?"

"Sure," Nikki said coolly.

Luke pulled his backpack onto his lap and started to look for the CD. "Today at lunch Suzanne told me—"

"Suzanne, Suzanne, Suzanne—that's all I ever hear from you lately!" Nikki exploded.

Luke stared at Nikki, clearly stunned. "I thought you liked her."

"I like her," Nikki said, turning the key in the ignition. "But not as much as you do."

"What does that mean?"

"What do you think?"

"You think I like her as a girlfriend?" Luke asked. "What gave you that idea?"

"Lots of things!"

"Such as?"

"Well, Victoria said—"

"Victoria!" Luke suddenly broke into a smile. "Nikki, come on. You know how Victoria is."

"No," Nikki said coldly, continuing to drive toward home. "How is she?"

"Well, for one thing, she's jealous," Luke said. "Remember how Victoria acted last week when Suzanne went out with John? She practically dug her fingernails in Suzanne's back. And now *you've* decided you like Suzanne. That must really piss Victoria off."

"So you're saying you're not interested in Suzanne?" Nikki asked.

"I swear I'm not."

Nikki put her hand on Luke's leg.

Luke stroked her shoulder. "What's the matter?"

"It's just that everything has been so weird between us lately," Nikki admitted. "It seems like we're constantly fighting—and I don't even know why."

Luke tilted her face up toward his. "I'll tell you why. It's because I've been crazy worrying about my mother lately. I've probably been taking it out on you. But you know what?"

"What?"

"I'm going to stop," Luke promised.

"Oh, Luke, I don't mind if you're upset about your mother. I just want us to be happy—like we used to be."

"We will," Luke said forcefully.

Nine

"So, my long-lost son comes home at last," Luke's mother slurred when he walked into their apartment later that afternoon.

Luke fought back a wave of disgust as he spotted his mother sitting at the kitchen table, a half-empty bottle of gin in front of her. The room reeked of alcohol and stale smoke.

"How was school today?" Mrs. Martinson asked.

"How was *work* today?" Luke shot back, throwing his books onto the coffee table. "Or didn't you go?"

An ugly looked passed over Mrs. Martinson's face. She picked up the bottle and swallowed another mouthful.

Luke didn't care if his mother ignored him. He already knew she hadn't gone to work. It was only four-thirty in the afternoon. If she'd gone to work, she wouldn't have gotten home until after five-thirty. Luke felt rage race around in circles in his stomach, demanding a way out. He wanted to knock over chairs, break dishes, scream. "You got fired, didn't you?" he asked quietly.

"No." Mrs. Martinson was suddenly belligerent. "I quit! I couldn't wait to get out of there. My boss—ha! The jerk. What a quack! He isn't even a real doctor, but that didn't stop him from thinking he could tell me what to do."

"Mom, he was your *boss!*"

"That doesn't make him better than me," Mrs. Martinson sneered.

Luke snorted. "Do you know what today's date is?"

Mrs. Martinson shook her head and took another gulp of gin. "No, but I bet you're about to tell me, smart boy."

"That's right," Luke said with quiet fury. "It's September twenty-second."

"So?"

"So you still haven't paid the rent for August!" Luke yelled. "What are you going to tell the landlord? That your boss bossed you around too much?"

"Don't talk to me like that," Mrs. Martinson said in a threatening tone.

Luke took a deep breath. "We're going to get kicked out of here," he said as calmly as he could.

Mrs. Martinson made a face. "I bet that would be real embarrassing for you, wouldn't it?"

"Embarrassing?" Luke repeated. "What are you talking about?"

"About you!" his mother taunted. "You're afraid your rich little girlfriend won't want to be seen with you anymore, aren't you?"

"Nikki isn't like that!" Luke yelled.

"Isn't she?"

"No!" Luke stormed out of the kitchen.

"Why don't you get your precious princess to pay the rent?" Mrs. Martinson yelled after him.

Luke slammed his bedroom door and slumped against it. His mother had been a drunk for a long time, but lately she had gotten worse. Luke didn't know how to handle her anymore.

Dinnertime came and went. When it got dark, Luke crawled into bed, trying to remember when things had gone so wrong with his mother. He knew it hadn't always been this way—he had vague memories of himself as a little boy playing in the sun-filled backyard of his parents' house. It had been a world of tricycles and toys and laughter.

Luke's mother hadn't fallen apart when they first learned of his father's illness. She'd been strong and sober the entire time he'd been sick, and for a while after he died. Luke couldn't remember one specific day when she had suddenly changed. It had happened slowly, gradually. Maybe she'd started with a drink in the evenings to help numb her loneliness.

By the time the first weak sunlight filtered in

his window, Luke had realized there was only one important person in his life: Nikki. And he couldn't afford to lose her.

"Hey, what's up? Nice shirt," Suzanne said to Luke as she slid into a seat at their usual lunch table the next day. Suzanne was only the second person to arrive, but she chose a seat diagonally across from him. She didn't want to sit too close to him.

Luke glanced down at his faded black concert T-shirt. The shirt was so worn, the logo wasn't visible anymore. "It's one of my favorites," he commented.

"It must be. Otherwise you wouldn't be caught dead in something so beat up." Suzanne smiled, and the corners of her eyes crinkled up.

Even though he felt lousy, Luke found himself smiling back at her.

Victoria and Nikki came up. Nikki was wearing a white shirt that showed off her late-summer tan and a pair of jeans that hugged her hips, making her irresistible to Luke.

"Hi," Nikki said, claiming the seat next to Luke.

"Hi," Luke said sleepily. He put his arm around Nikki and gave her a tight bear hug.

Victoria glanced from Luke to Suzanne as she took the top off her yogurt. "You two looked awfully chummy when we got here. What were you talking about?"

Suzanne and Luke exchanged looks, and

started to laugh. Luke couldn't believe Nikki didn't seem to notice how conniving her best friend was. It was refreshing that Suzanne obviously saw through Victoria's scheming.

"I was just admiring Luke's stunning wardrobe," Suzanne joked.

"Maybe I could take you shopping sometime," Luke said with mock formality. "You know, to serve as your consultant." He turned to Nikki with a smile.

But Nikki wasn't smiling, and neither was Victoria. Luke immediately knew what the problem was: he was being too friendly with Suzanne. Nikki had already let him know how jealous that made her, and their playful conversation probably wasn't helping convince Nikki that he loved her and only her.

"Hey, guys." Keith spun a chair around, sat down, and started to complain about Mr. Roberts, his math teacher.

Luke took a bite of his sandwich and wondered what he could do to reassure Nikki.

"I'm never going to pass that test next week," Keith moaned. "And once my B average is blown, I'm history on the football field."

"If you need help, give me a call," Suzanne offered, putting down the apple she'd been eating. "Math is one of my best subjects."

"Really?" Keith sounded interested.

Suddenly seeing his chance, Luke smirked at Suzanne. "So, Suzanne, you sure do move fast.

You've figured out your next move already, haven't you?"

"Move?" Suzanne repeated. "What are you talking about?"

Luke licked his lips. "First you latched on to John and then dumped him when you were finished with him. Now you're trying to latch on to Keith."

Victoria's eyebrows flew up.

Keith frowned.

"Luke . . ." Nikki sounded disapproving.

"That's not true," Suzanne said weakly. "I was just trying to help. . . ." Tears pooled in Suzanne's eyes, and the sight made Luke feel sick to his stomach.

"Besides," Keith said lightly, "I wouldn't mind if she did use me."

Luke shrugged. "Oh, well, then I guess I was wrong. Sorry, Suzanne."

There was a long silence at the table.

"So," Keith said to break the ice, "it's finally Friday. What's everybody up to this weekend?"

Suzanne swallowed hard, clearly still fighting tears. "My mom's studio opens tomorrow. You're all invited to the grand opening. Bring anyone you want."

"We should all go together," Nikki suggested.

"Not me," Luke said quickly. "I have to work."

"I'll go," Victoria said.

The conversation continued for the next twenty minutes. Suzanne told everyone about the different classes at Willis Workout, and Nikki asked all sorts of questions.

Luke couldn't wait for lunch to end. He got through it only by concentrating on the way Nikki rubbed his knee under the table—and by ignoring Suzanne's sad face. As hard as it was, he knew he had done the right thing. He had given Nikki the reassurance she needed. Right now, that was all that mattered.

Nikki thought about Luke during all of her afternoon classes. She hadn't liked the way he'd attacked Suzanne at lunch. But after the terrible week of doubt she'd experienced, it *had* been reassuring.

Luke and Nikki had plans to hang out at her house and watch a video that afternoon. Nikki hurried toward Luke's locker immediately after her last class. She couldn't wait for their date to begin.

When Luke saw her, he smiled in a hungry way, making her heart flip-flop. "Hi."

"Hi."

Luke closed his locker softly and took Nikki's hand.

"Where are we going?" she asked as he led her down the hall. "The parking lot is in the other direction."

"We're not going to the parking lot," Luke told her. He stopped at the end of the deserted hallway, which led to a rarely used stairwell. He slipped his arms around her waist and softly kissed her neck.

A delicious shiver ran from Nikki's shoulders to her fingertips. She wrapped her arms around Luke. He gave her a warm, soft kiss on the lips. Nikki had never wanted to be kissed more—and it had never felt better. She backed against the wall and Luke followed, pressing up against her. She kissed him more urgently.

They had been there for quite a while when someone started down the stairway. "Oh—sorry!"

Nikki's eyes flew open, but the intruder had already fled.

"Don't worry," Luke murmured. "It was only Keith."

Nikki felt a blush sweeping up her face. She wasn't embarrassed to give Luke a quick kiss in public or anything like that, but Keith had just witnessed a major public display of affection.

Luke smiled at her softly and gave her a kiss on the nose. "Want to go home?"

"Definitely," Nikki told him. "We'll have more privacy there."

Keith slammed through the door of the boys' locker room. A spasm of anger overcame him, and he punched one of the lockers. *Bam! Bam!* The pain in his fist helped Keith calm down. It wasn't easy walking in on Luke and Nikki in the middle of a major make-out session. It's just not fair, he thought.

"Hey, Stein, you okay?" John called.

"Yeah, yeah, I'm fine," Keith muttered, examining his already-swelling hand. He thought about what Luke had told him that afternoon: his mother had quit her job again. Keith felt the anger let go of him. Luke didn't have it easy. It wasn't right of Keith to want the only good thing in his life—the girl of both their dreams. Nikki.

Ten

"Hey, Suzanne!" Tim, the guy her mother had hired to work the juice bar, was waving at her.

Suzanne hurried over to him. "What's up?"

"I'm almost out of cups," he told her. "And carrots. Could you tell your mother for me?"

"Sure," Suzanne said, then went in search of her mother in the crowded gym.

Suddenly the door to the main studio flew open, and groups of sweaty people emerged. The last ones out were Nikki, Deb, Victoria, and John.

Nikki spotted Suzanne and waved.

"Hey!" Suzanne called. "How was class? You guys just came out of Funky Step, right?"

Nikki nodded. "It was exhausting."

"No joke!" Deb put in.

John rolled his eyes. "It was a piece of cake. Nothing compared to what Coach Kostro puts the team through every day."

Suzanne smiled at John. Despite their rocky start, at least they could still talk to each other.

"Well, the rest of us thought the class was pretty great," Deb said. "Right, Victoria?"

"It was okay."

Deb rolled her eyes. "A minute ago you said you loved it."

"Well, the instructor was pretty good," Victoria said.

"A minute ago you said she was the best instructor you've ever had," Deb said to Victoria, and then winked at Suzanne.

Suzanne smiled back. "I'll tell my mom you guys liked her. If you're looking for a really hard class, though, you should take one of Mom's. They're killers!"

"Hey, let's get something to drink," John suggested. "And then I want to hit the weights."

"The drinks at the juice bar are on the house today," Suzanne told the others as she pointed the way.

"Are you coming?" Nikki asked her.

"No, I've got to find my mom."

Nikki turned to John, Deb, and Victoria. "I'll catch up with you guys later. I'm keeping Suzanne company for a while."

Victoria frowned. She looked as if she was going to say something, but Deb took her arm and led her toward the juice bar before she could speak. "See you guys later," Deb said over her shoulder.

John followed behind them.

"Let's look for your mom in the weight room," Nikki suggested. "I saw some really cute guys headed that way."

"Okay," Suzanne agreed. "Isn't it cool how many men showed up today?"

"Well, I wish there were more," Nikki said. "John was the only guy in Funky Step."

"I'm glad he stayed in the class. Didn't he feel weird being the only guy?" Suzanne asked.

"John?" Nikki laughed. "No way. He was probably counting on being the only guy. Did you see that little black tank top he was wearing? And I swear he oiled his skin before he got here."

"Did all the girls sneak a peek at his bulging muscles?" Suzanne asked.

Nikki nodded. "You've got to admit—"

"They do look good," Suzanne finished.

"Exactly," Nikki said with a smile.

The girls saw a couple of young guys lifting free weights in the weight room. But Suzanne's attention was drawn to a group of older men and women conversing in the corner. A man with thick salt-and-pepper hair was talking in a booming voice. He was wearing workout clothes, but he didn't look as if he'd broken a sweat.

"Who are you looking at?" Nikki put her head next to Suzanne's and followed her gaze. "Oh— that's Mr. Hill. Victoria's dad."

"He's really attracted an audience," Suzanne commented.

"That's because he practically runs the town,"

Nikki said, taking a step away from Suzanne. "He's president of the town council and owns most of downtown. You can't go anywhere without tripping over him."

"Yuck," Suzanne said.

"Don't worry," Nikki told her. "You're too young to vote, so you're safe for another couple of years. But he's going to love your mom. Local businesswoman and all that."

"I'll have to warn her." Suzanne turned away from the weight room.

"You should," Nikki said as she followed her out to the hall. "Don't tell Victoria I told you this, but her father's favorite sport is a cocktail marathon."

"That's terrible."

Nikki shrugged. "Plenty of people around here booze it up. It's almost expected. Hey, isn't that your mom?" She pointed toward the door of the dressing room.

"Yeah," Suzanne said. "But the question is, who's she with?"

Valerie Willis, wearing a red leotard with spaghetti straps and a matching wraparound skirt, her long brown hair up in a twist, was standing next to the dressing room door. She was chatting with a handsome man who was wearing shorts and a faded Rhode Island School of Design T-shirt. His comfy-looking clothes were a bit out of place, but he didn't seem to notice.

"That's Mr. Houghton," Nikki told her. "You

met his son, Ian, at school. He's a senior."

"Hmm," Suzanne said. "He's not bad for an old guy."

"You can say that again. And Ian's not hard to look at, either."

The girls approached the couple.

"Hi, honey!" Valerie Willis sounded happy. "Suzanne, I want you to meet Mr. Houghton."

"Hi," Suzanne said. "Mom, this is my friend, Nikki. She drove me to the concert last weekend."

"Oh, hi, Nikki. It's nice to meet you," Ms. Willis said.

Mr. Houghton gave Suzanne a warm smile. "Welcome to Hillcrest."

"Thanks. Oh, I've got some bad news, Mom," Suzanne said. "Tim's running out of cups and carrots."

"Well, we can't have that!" She turned to Mr. Houghton. "It was wonderful meeting you. I hope we can talk again soon, but I'd better go take care of this carrot crisis before it gets out of hand."

"Good luck. I know how difficult carrots can be. And congratulations on the gym. I'll see you around."

After the adults had wandered off, Suzanne and Nikki exchanged amused looks. "My mom certainly doesn't waste any time."

Deb came out of the dressing room. "Hey, you guys!"

"Hey. Where's Victoria?" Nikki asked.

Deb rolled her eyes. "Back in class. She's taking step aerobics this time."

"And you didn't join her?" Suzanne asked.

"No way," Deb said with a groan. "One class is more than enough for me. My muscles are killing me."

"Want to try out the new whirlpool before you leave? I'm dying to go," Suzanne said.

"That would be so cool, but I didn't bring my bathing suit," Deb said.

"Me neither," Nikki said.

"No problem," Suzanne said. "Mom has a bunch of extras stashed in the office. We can use those."

"I'm there," Deb said.

A few minutes later, the girls were soaking up the warm water in the egg-shaped whirlpool.

"This is heaven," Deb said.

"Mmm," Nikki sighed as she closed her eyes and slipped deeper into the water.

Suzanne was relaxed, too, but it didn't have much to do with the warm bubbles. She felt terrific because she was finally making real friends. It was time to accept that she and her mom were staying here in Hillcrest, like it or not. And Suzanne couldn't help being psyched about Willis Workout. Her mother had told her they'd already sold dozens of one-year memberships and hundreds of class cards. So what if her mother had gone into debt to build the place? She'd probably be able to pay back her loans soon. Maybe she'd even be able to buy Suzanne a car to drive to school. . . .

Twenty minutes later the girls got out of the whirlpool. By the time they'd dried off, changed their clothes, and gone back to the main floor, the crowd had thinned out.

"Look," Nikki said, pointing to a woman near the door. "There's my mom."

"Really?" Suzanne said. "Can I meet her?"

"Sure," Nikki said.

"Nikki!" Mrs. Stewart called as the girls approached her. "Where have you been? I've been looking all over for you."

"We were in the whirlpool."

Mrs. Stewart raised her eyebrows. "Whirlpool? That sounds like heaven. Just what I need after a long day at the station."

"You'd better get a membership," Nikki told her mom.

Mrs. Stewart patted her purse. "Already did. Now, come on, honey. We've got to get home."

"First I want you to meet my new friend, Suzanne Willis. Her mom owns this place."

"Hi," Suzanne said.

Everybody knew Mrs. Stewart was the host of *Open Your Eyes,* an early-morning news show. Suzanne's grandmother watched her show every morning. In fact, it was a family joke. Suzanne's mother hated the show as much as Suzanne's grandmother loved it. They were always arguing about it at the breakfast table.

"Nikki's told me a lot about you," Mrs. Stewart told Suzanne. "It's nice to meet you."

"This is so amazing," Suzanne said. "My grandma is going to flip when she hears I met you. She's a huge fan." Suzanne couldn't help but notice that Mrs. Stewart looked older in person than she did on TV. Her eyes were puffy with dark circles under them, and her hair looked dry. Suzanne knew Mrs. Stewart wasn't much older than her own mother, but the differences were like night and day.

"Thanks," Mrs. Stewart said. "It's always nice to hear about people who enjoy the show. And speaking of the show, we've got to hit the road, Nikki. We're having dinner with my boss."

Nikki groaned. "Thrillsville. Three hours of gossip about people I don't know."

"I'm glad I'm not you. Have fun," Suzanne said.

But before Nikki and Mrs. Stewart could leave, Suzanne's mother came up behind them. "Hello, I'm Valerie Willis," she said brightly. "Welcome to Willis Workout. Let me know if you have any questions about the club."

Mrs. Stewart smiled. "Thanks, but there's no need for a sales pitch. I've already signed up. I bought a year's membership."

Ms. Willis sighed. "That's great. I think I'm all pitched out."

"Mom," Suzanne said, "this is Helen Stewart—Nikki's mom."

"Oh—of course," Suzanne's mother said, an

expression of dislike immediately crossing her face. Her smile was quickly back in place, but not before Suzanne noticed the change. "I'm sorry I didn't recognize you sooner," Suzanne's mother continued. "I've seen your show hundreds of times."

"Oh, that's okay," Mrs. Stewart said. "Without my makeup on, I look like a different person."

"Not at all," Ms. Willis said. "You're just as lovely in person. And I'm honored to have you as a member of my club."

Suzanne detected an insincere note in her mother's voice. Was it just because she didn't like *Open Your Eyes?*

"I gave you a twenty," the blond woman snapped.

A moment passed. "What?" Luke asked, confused.

The woman thrust out her hand. There was a dollar and some coins in it. "I gave you a twenty," she repeated. "You owe me another ten."

Luke forced himself to focus on what was going on. He'd been so distracted by his mom and money problems that he'd put the woman's money away before checking that he was giving her the right amount of change. "Oh, I'm sorry. I—I wasn't thinking about what I was doing. I'm having a crappy day."

The woman's face softened. "Bad days are something I can relate to. Sorry I jumped at you like that."

Luke bit his lip. Why was he telling customers about his problems? It was pitiful. "Listen, it was my mistake," he said. "Just let me go to the back and get the register key."

"Key?" the woman asked.

"Yeah," Luke said. "If I haven't made a sale, I can't open the register without the key."

"If it would be easier, I could come back when Rick is here."

Rick was Luke's boss, and lots of customers knew him by name. He was a friendly guy who loved music and was an authority on recordings of all genres. Rick was Mr. Good Mood. And no wonder—the Tunesmith was the most popular record store in Hillcrest. Rick was raking in the bucks, and he'd just bought a new powerboat.

"It's really not a big deal," Luke told the woman. "I'll be right back." He came around the counter, walked back to Rick's office, and let himself in. He opened the top desk drawer and took out the register key. A moment later he was back behind the counter. He turned the key in the register, and the drawer opened with a ping. Luke pulled out a ten-dollar bill and handed it to the woman.

"Thanks," she said. "Try to enjoy the rest of your weekend."

"Uh, sure," Luke said. "You, too."

The bell on the door jingled as the woman left.

Luke couldn't remember if she'd really given him a twenty. She probably had. Most people in

Hillcrest were honest. Besides, it didn't really matter. Rick had told Luke never to argue with a customer. If they complained about their change, he was supposed to assume they were right. After closing that night, the register would print out a total of the day's sales, and Luke would compare it with the money in the drawer. If the drawer was short, Luke would explain to Rick. Rick always said five or ten dollars here and there weren't worth losing a customer.

"Excuse me?" Two girls who looked as if they were about eleven years old stood in front of the counter. "Do you have the new Madonna CD?"

"Sure. It's in the second row," Luke said, pointing them in the right direction.

"Thanks." The girls walked across the store, whispering to each other. One of them had hair the same shade as Nikki's.

Nikki. The thought of her reminded Luke of his mother's words from the night before. "Your rich little girlfriend . . . Why don't you get your precious princess to pay the rent?" Luke needed a better way to make money, and fast. Now that his mom had lost yet another job, Luke was going to have to come up with a way to pay the rent himself.

"Could you tell us how much this will be with tax?" One of the girls interrupted his thoughts, holding out the Madonna CD to him.

"We're not sure we have enough money," the other girl added.

Luke winked at them. "No problem." He took

a calculator out from under the counter, punched in the price, and added the sales tax. "It will be twelve forty-seven altogether," he told the girls.

Luke waited while they counted their money. First both girls pulled the bills out of their wallets. Then they dumped a pile of change onto the counter. Their faces grew more serious as they counted. After a brief, whispered conference, the blond scooped up all the money and said, "We don't have enough."

The girls' disappointed faces made Luke feel even worse than he had before. "How much is not enough?" he asked.

"Almost a dollar," one of the girls said.

Luke considered. "I'll tell you what. Give me what you have. Then the next time you get your allowances, bring in the rest."

The blond kid's eyes were wide. "Seriously?"

"Sure," Luke said. "My boss is a rich guy. I don't think he'll miss a dollar."

"Wow," the other girl said. "This is totally great. Thanks."

"No problem," Luke said as he took the CD from the girls and ran it over the scanner. The cash register pinged open. Luke reached for the girls' money, but when he saw the pile of change on the counter, he made a face. He couldn't deal with all those pennies and nickels, so he just ignored the money, put the CD in a bag, and handed it to the blond girl.

"Thank you, mister," she said.

"Yeah, thanks a ton," her friend chimed in.

"Let's go to my house," the blond kid said to her friend, walking toward the front door. "I want to listen to this right away."

After the girls had gone, Luke gathered up their money and counted it into the register. He felt a sudden pang of doubt. Should he have given the CD to the girls? It seemed like the right thing to do at the time, but maybe he shouldn't have been so generous with someone else's money. Luke decided to write a note to explain to Rick. He left the register open while he searched for a piece of paper.

As Luke sat down to write, his coworker, Mark, came out of the stockroom. "You okay out here?" he asked.

"Yeah, why?" Luke said.

"I'm taking my break," Mark announced. "Want anything to eat?"

"No, thanks," Luke said, thinking about his penniless state.

"I'll be back in an hour." And out the door he went.

After Mark left, Luke glanced down and read his note to Rick, then balled the paper up. He was making too big a deal out of a small thing. After all, what he'd told the girls was true. Rick wouldn't miss the dollar. Besides, it was a loan. When the girls got their allowances, they'd bring in the difference.

Luke started to push the register drawer

closed, but then his eye fell on the neat stack of twenties inside. If Rick wouldn't miss a dollar, would he miss a twenty? Or a couple of twenties? Forty dollars might be enough to keep the landlord off their backs for a few days. . . .

The front bell jingled, interrupting Luke's dishonest thoughts. An older man with a little boy in tow headed for the classical music section.

Luke slammed the register closed. This is crazy, he told himself. The last thing he needed was to lose his job.

A few minutes later the man and boy came up to the counter. The man handed Luke a boxed set of Mozart CDs.

Luke turned the box over every which way and was annoyed to see that it didn't have a bar code.

"Daddy," the little boy whined, tugging at his father's jacket, "I lost my bear."

The man sighed. "You must have dropped it in the aisle." He looked at Luke. "We'll be right back." With that, he took the boy's hand and turned away from the counter.

"No problem." Luke started to punch the price into the register. But while the man searched for the missing bear, Luke hesitated. If I don't ring up this sale, Rick will never know the money is missing, Luke thought as he glanced down at the boxed set. It cost over forty bucks—more than enough to calm the landlord down. He quickly pulled out the calculator and figured the tax. As the man approached the

116

counter, Luke put the CDs in a bag and stapled it shut with shaky hands.

"Okay, what do I owe you?" the man asked.

"Forty-six oh one," Luke read off the calculator. Then, with a jolt, he realized if he made change out of the register, the cash drawer would come up short that amount. If he gave this man ninety-nine cents change, he'd have to find a way to replace it before Mark came back. "Don't worry about the penny," Luke added quickly.

"Great," the man said, handing him three twenties.

Luke stared at the money in his hand. He still had to make change, and the register was locked. Luke's heart was pounding in his chest. Then he remembered the register key, sitting right next to the calculator on the shelf.

"Daddy, I have to go to the bathroom," the little boy announced.

The man looked down. "Just a minute, Alec."

Luke picked up the key, opened the register, and handed the man fourteen dollars. He felt faint—probably because he was hardly breathing. What if the man noticed something was up? What if he asked for a receipt?

"Daddy, I have to go *now*," Alec demanded.

"Just a minute," his father repeated impatiently, putting the change in his wallet.

Luke held out the bag. "Thank you."

The man took the bag and motioned toward

the door. "Come on," he said to Alec. "Let's get you to the rest room."

Luke watched them walk out, then glanced down at the still-open register. The drawer was now fourteen dollars short. Luke slipped one of the man's twenties into the register and took out six ones. He stuffed the ones and the man's two other twenties into his pocket and slammed the register shut.

It would have taken Luke a week to earn forty-six dollars working part-time for minimum wage. He wiped his hands on his jeans and took a deep breath. I'm never doing this again, he swore to himself.

Later that evening Valerie Willis stood inside Willis Workout and locked the front door. "Whew! That was quite a day."

Suzanne nodded. "You should be proud of yourself, Mom."

"You know what?" Her mother put her arm around Suzanne's shoulders as they started toward the back office. "I *am* proud. And not just of Willis Workout. I'm proud of you. You were a big help today."

"No problem," Suzanne said.

"Well, I think we should celebrate by going out to dinner," Ms. Willis said. "What are you in the mood for?"

"Hmm . . . Something fattening. All I've done today is watch people work out and drink carrot juice."

Ms. Willis laughed as she unlocked the office. "Pizza?"

Suzanne nodded. "With pepperoni."

"Deal," Ms. Willis agreed. With a sigh, she sank down in her desk chair and pulled the cash drawer from the main register toward her.

The doorbell rang, and Suzanne jumped. She hadn't even known there *was* a doorbell at the studio.

Ms. Willis groaned. "I wonder who that can be."

"Probably someone who desperately needs a multiple-class card," Suzanne joked.

"Well, they'll have to come back," Ms. Willis said. "We're all sold out."

"I'll get it," Suzanne offered as she turned toward the door.

"Thanks, honey," Ms. Willis said. "I've got to do the receipts before we leave, anyway."

Suzanne walked out into the darkened gym and crossed to the front door. She peeked through the window in the door and saw a man standing on the step, holding a very long rectangular box. Only one thing could fit into that box: roses. She unlocked the door.

"Valerie Willis?" the delivery man asked.

"No, but I can take those for her," Suzanne said, holding her arms out to take the box. "She's my mom." Who's sending Mom roses? she wondered.

"Great." The delivery man handed the flowers to Suzanne.

"Don't you want me to sign something?" Suzanne asked.

"No need." He was already halfway down the stairs.

"Look what you got!" Suzanne said, walking back into the office.

Her mother's eyes widened. "Roses? Wow!"

Suzanne put the box down on the table. Her mother took off the top and pushed aside the tissue paper. The roses inside were blood-red and perfect.

"They're fantastic!" Suzanne said. "Who are they from?"

"Let's see," her mother said, opening the tiny white envelope nestled among the flowers and reading the card inside. Her happy expression turned stone cold, and she dropped the card on the desk. Suzanne leaned forward and saw that the card was blank except for the letter *S*.

"S? Who's S?" Suzanne asked.

"I—I don't know," her mother said. "I have no idea."

"Then why did you get that look on your face when you read the card?" Suzanne pressed.

Her mother sat back down in her chair. She didn't answer for a long moment. "I just hoped the flowers were from someone else," she finally admitted.

Suzanne was skeptical. "Who?"

"Someone I met today," Ms. Willis said.

"Mr. Houghton?" Suzanne asked.

"Right," Ms. Willis said, her expression brightening. "He seems like a nice man. And don't you think he's handsome?"

Suzanne rarely got to see this giggly, girlish side of her mother. She liked it. Sure, her mom went out on lots of dates, but this time it was different. She actually seemed interested in this guy. "Definitely."

Ms. Willis stood up. "Come on, let's get that pizza."

"What about the receipts?"

"I'll take care of them in the morning," Ms. Willis said.

As Suzanne followed her mother to the door, she caught sight of the card again. She couldn't help thinking her mother was hiding something. But she decided to drop the subject of S for the time being. She wanted to let her mom enjoy her success—and her new crush.

Eleven

"Where were you at lunch today?" Nikki asked Victoria on Monday afternoon. French, their last class of the day, was about to begin.

"I ate with Katia," Victoria said. "I saw you two lovebirds sitting together, and I figured you could use some time alone."

"Lovebirds?" Nikki repeated. "I ate lunch with Suzanne."

"Well, who did you think I meant?" Victoria asked innocently.

Nikki rolled her eyes. "I wish you'd lay off Suzanne."

"If I want to see you, I don't have much choice, do I?" Victoria asked darkly. "You and I'm-from-the-big-city-so-adore-me Suzanne are practically joined at the hip these days. What did you talk about at lunch? How great Hillcrest is?"

"What are you talking about? Suzanne doesn't

even want to live here. She'd much rather be back in Brooklyn. And who can blame her? At least New York City is exciting," Nikki said.

"Oh, forget it," Victoria said. "If you want to be taken in by Suzanne, fine. Just don't ask me to be that stupid."

Nikki turned away from Victoria and opened her book. But a second later she turned back. "What's your problem? Do you still think Suzanne's trying to steal Luke away from me?"

Victoria shrugged. "I wouldn't put it past her."

"That's ridiculous!" Nikki exclaimed. She glanced over her shoulder and leaned closer to Victoria. "Luke's made it pretty clear he isn't interested in her," she added in a low voice.

"Yeah," Victoria began. "Isn't that convenient?"

Nikki looked disgusted. She turned back to her book and started to review verbs.

Victoria told herself she didn't care. So what if her best friend was spending every waking moment with Suzanne? Victoria was busy, anyway, working on her favorite project: Ian.

The two weeks Nikki had given Victoria to get a date with him would be up at lunchtime the next afternoon. Victoria wasn't even sure if the bet was still on, since Nikki hadn't mentioned it in over a week. She'd probably been too busy playing with her new friend. At this point, Victoria wasn't planning to mention the bet, either, since it seemed as if she was going to lose. Not that she was planning to give up. She still had almost twenty-four hours to work on Ian, and she was going to make every second count.

As class began Victoria considered when she should run into Ian next. She had his entire schedule memorized, so she could arrange a "chance" meeting anytime during the day. Unfortunately, lunch was always a waste—Ian had gotten into the habit of eating with his cousin Sally, reason enough to avoid him then. Between classes was tough, since they had only five minutes to get from one room to the next. Victoria was good, but it was practically impossible to seduce someone while running down the hallway. Before and after school were the best times, as long as Sally wasn't around. Victoria decided she would offer Ian a ride home that afternoon. She happened to know his car was in the shop. Now, if only this stupid class would end . . .

About an hour later, Victoria spotted Ian walking down the street, and she pulled her car over to the curb. He glanced toward her, then away, and continued walking.

Victoria leaned out the open window. "Want a ride?"

"Sure. Thanks." Ian jumped in on the passenger side, and Victoria took off again.

"What are you reading?" Victoria pointed to a scuffed-up book he was holding.

"Baudelaire," Ian said. *"Les Fleurs du Mal."*

"Who's Bau . . . ?"

"Baudelaire," Ian helped her out. "He's a French poet."

"Is that for school?" Victoria asked as she braked for a yellow light. Normally she would have zoomed through the intersection, but she wanted to make this ride last as long as possible.

Ian laughed. "No. The title means 'Flowers of Evil.' It's a bit, well, deep for school."

Victoria felt a prick of annoyance. This conversation was making her feel stupid. She read plenty of books, even some that weren't required for school. But French poetry about evil flowers? Come on!

"Why are you reading that?" Victoria asked.

"A friend recommended it," Ian said.

Victoria's eyes widened. "A friend from school?" She couldn't imagine anyone at Hillcrest High reading poetry for fun. Not even the Geek Guild.

"No," Ian said. "Someone I met online."

"Isn't talking to someone online kind of impersonal?" she asked, her hand "accidentally" touching Ian's leg when she went to shift to another gear. "Wouldn't you rather be talking to someone who's really there?"

"The people online *are* really there," Ian said in his even tone. It was the tone he always used with her.

Victoria felt like punching him. Other guys noticed her. Other guys flirted with her. Why not Ian? Didn't the guy have hormones? Maybe he

125

really *wasn't* interested in her. . . . But something told Victoria that wasn't the problem. She just had to try harder.

"I don't understand," Victoria said in a clueless voice most guys found irresistible. "How can you meet people online? How does it work?"

"Well, there are these things called forums," Ian explained. "Each one is on a different topic. One of my favorites is on the Beat writers and poets."

The Beat writers and poets? Victoria repeated to herself. That sounds kind of twisted.

Her confusion must have shown on her face, because Ian said, "Don't tell me you don't know about the Beats! They're the best. You know, Allen Ginsberg, Jack Kerouac . . ."

Victoria gave a little shrug.

Ian shook his head. "Well, the forum can be on anything—old cars or Valhalla or Chinese cooking. Hey, that's my house right there." He pointed to a stark white house that stood out from the others on the street.

"What a great place." Victoria was happy to change the subject.

"My dad designed it," Ian told her. "He's an architect."

"That's so cool," Victoria said as she pulled into the Houghtons' driveway. She half expected Ian to jump out as soon as the car stopped. She was psyched when he didn't.

"I found this totally amazing place online last

weekend," Ian told her, finally a bit of excitement in his voice. "It's modeled after a nightclub and doesn't open until ten every night. I've been hanging out there a lot lately. It's called the Cyberlounge."

Victoria smiled slyly. "I love clubs! Of course, I've never been to one that's on a computer before. It sounds outrageous."

"You should try it sometime," Ian said.

"I'd love to," Victoria said with all the enthusiasm she could muster. "Too bad I don't have a computer at home. . . ." She let her voice trail off, hoping Ian would pick up on the hint. In truth, her father had a state-of-the-art PC gathering dust in his office. He'd probably raise her allowance if she ever turned it on.

"Well, thanks for the ride." Ian started to get out of the car.

Victoria considered screaming. Maybe that would get Ian's attention. Instead she forced her voice to sound casual. "Could we go to the Cyberlounge together sometime? You could introduce me to your friends."

"Sure," Ian said with a shrug.

"How about this weekend?" Victoria asked.

"I guess I could do that."

"Saturday?" Victoria pressed.

"Saturday," Ian agreed as he climbed out. "Come by at ten."

She had a date with Ian! Finally. And she

knew just what she was going to wear. Nikki's leather jacket. No, make that *her* leather jacket.

Keith offered John a ride home after football practice the next afternoon. They were just pulling out of the student parking lot when a voice called out, "Hey, Keith, wait up! I need a ride!"

Keith glanced into his rearview mirror for the briefest moment. But he didn't slow down.

John twisted around and looked out the back window. "Keith, that's Katia."

"So?"

"So you can't abandon your little sister."

"Why not?"

"Because I said so," John told him. "Give the kid a break."

Keith groaned, but he slowed the car to a stop.

Katia hurried up to the black Corvette. John got out so she could squeeze into the backseat that wasn't really a seat at all. The sports car had been designed for two. The little ledge Katia perched on had been intended as a place to store a picnic lunch or a pair of sunglasses, not a person.

"I'm so glad I caught you," Katia told Keith breathlessly. "For a minute I thought you didn't hear me."

John and Keith exchanged looks.

Keith put the car in gear and zoomed out of the parking lot.

"So, is everything set for tonight?" John asked Keith.

"Yep," Keith replied.

"What's all set?" Katia asked, leaning forward to listen to the conversation.

"None of your business."

"Oh, come on," she said. "You guys can tell me."

"It's not a big deal," John told her. "Just that Keith talked us into playing poker with him again."

Keith shot John a sharp look. The way Keith felt, the less his little sister knew about his business, the better.

"Seriously? I thought you guys swore off poker."

Keith thought back to the day he and John had arrived at practice late after serving detention. Coach Kostro had been furious, yelling at them in front of the entire team for ten minutes. Then he'd sent everyone on a three-mile run—in their uniforms and gear. By the time the coach calmed down, the other players had been ready to kill them.

It had taken Keith two whole weeks to convince his friends to play cards again. John was the last to agree.

"This is nothing like that," Keith said quickly. He didn't want to give John a chance to change his mind. "We're playing at our house. As far as I know, Mom and Dad don't have any rules against playing cards."

129

Katia chuckled. "No, they actually seem to like it."

"Well, it doesn't matter, anyway. They're going to some benefit tonight," Keith told her.

"I'm inviting someone, then," Katia announced.

"No way. I'm not having a party for your friends. In fact, I don't remember inviting *you.*"

"Why would you have to invite me to my own house?" Katia asked sweetly.

John laughed. "She's got you there, man. Besides, you told me we had room for one more player."

"I didn't mean *her,*" Keith said.

"Isn't Ian bringing Sally?" John asked.

"Yeah. So?" Keith asked.

"So she won't want to be the only girl," John said.

"Right," Katia put in.

Keith pulled up in front of John's house. "Fine. Katia can come," he gave in.

"What a sweet big brother you are," John said as he got out of the Corvette. "Catch you guys later. Thanks for the ride."

Katia climbed into the front seat. "Thanks so much, Keith. This is going to be fun."

Keith was totally annoyed as he turned the car toward home. Not only didn't he want Katia to come, he hadn't liked the way she and John had teamed up against him.

Later, when Keith saw what Katia put on for the game—tight jeans and a low-cut red

130

T-shirt—he almost laughed at his little sister. Suddenly her interest in his poker game made sense. He wondered which of his friends she had a crush on. Not that it mattered. None of them would stoop to dating a lowly sophomore. Especially since the sophomore was his little sister.

"I'll get it," Katia called when the doorbell rang.

"No, *I* will," Keith said. "It's my party, remember?"

"Sorry," Katia said, walking back to the family room.

Keith opened the door. It was John. His hair was damp, and he was wearing a clean white oxford shirt.

"Hey, man," Keith greeted him. "Something stinks," he added, his nose wrinkling. "Are you wearing perfume?"

"Cologne," John corrected him.

"Why are you so dressed up?" Keith asked.

John grinned. "Nothing wrong with taking an interest in my personal hygiene."

Keith and John started toward the family room. They'd gotten only halfway when the doorbell rang again.

"I know my way," John said, and he continued on.

Keith doubled back to the door. It was Ian and Sally.

Sally was wearing a green eyeshade. "Do you

want us to check our weapons?" she asked around the cigar in her mouth.

"Huh?"

"Old West humor," Ian said in a stage whisper. "One of Sally's specialties."

"It's just that I don't want no trouble," she drawled. "You know, no shoot-outs or nothing like that."

"I don't think you have to worry about that," Keith said, leading his guests inside. "But my parents will freak if you light that cigar in the house."

"Light it?" Sally repeated in her own voice. "Are you crazy? Do you think I want to get cancer or something?"

Keith forced a laugh. He was beginning to wonder if it had been a mistake to let Ian invite Sally. The way she was carrying on, he could tell she'd never played poker before. He didn't feel like spending the night explaining the difference between a straight and a full house.

When the threesome got to the family room, John and Katia were huddled together in the corner, whispering. Keith almost laughed out loud. Good luck, little sister, he thought.

Everyone sat down at the round table in the family room. Katia chose a seat next to John.

Keith tapped the deck of cards against the table. "I'll deal first, okay?"

Everyone agreed.

"Let's play five-card draw," Keith suggested.

"Twos are wild. Does everyone know the rules?" He was surprised when they all nodded. "Okay, the ante will be fifty cents to start." Keith watched while everyone pushed two quarters into a pile in the middle of the table. Then he dealt the cards.

Katia looked at her cards and made a face. "I'll take five," she said, throwing them all down.

Keith groaned. "First of all, it's not your turn. Second of all, you can only discard three."

"Really?" Katia scooped her cards back up. "That stinks."

Keith rolled his eyes and turned to Ian. "How many, man?" he asked.

"Three." Ian put down three cards, and Keith dealt him three new ones.

"Sally?" Keith asked.

"One." Sally laid down one card decisively and picked up the one Keith dealt her.

Keith looked at Katia. "It's your turn now."

"What's better?" Katia asked. "Hearts or clubs?"

"It doesn't matter," Keith said impatiently.

"Hmm," Katia said. "One, please."

"But you wanted five before," Keith said.

"So I changed my mind," Katia said, placing one card on the table.

Keith handed his sister her card. Then he quickly glanced at his own hand, discarded two, and drew.

Ian started the bidding. Sally matched his

bet. Katia and John both dropped out. John immediately picked up Katia's hand and began pointing to cards and whispering advice to her.

Keith glanced at his hand. All he had was a crappy pair of nines. But he knew how easy it was to bluff Ian. "I'll see your bet, and raise it a dollar," Keith said, pushing a dollar and a quarter into the pot.

"I'm out," Ian said immediately, throwing his cards down.

Keith raised his eyebrows at Sally.

"I'll see you and raise you another dollar." Sally threw two dollars into the pot.

Keith smiled. He decided it *had* been a good idea to let Sally come. Or at least a lucrative one.

"I'll see you." He put in another dollar. "What do you have?"

"A pair of eights," Sally said, turning over her cards. "How about you?"

"A pair of nines. Close one," Keith said, scooping up his money. "Why did you raise your bet?"

"It's called bluffing," Sally said.

"Good try, Sally. But no one ever beats Keith," Ian said.

"Oh, well, there's a first time for everything. Maybe tonight's my lucky night."

"Listen, Sally, there's no need to kid yourself. You're not going to beat me. You're just a beginner," Keith said, impatiently putting the cards down in front of Ian. "Deal."

"Ooh," Katia said. "Keith thinks he's so great."

Sally looked surprised. "Hey, Keith, I'm not a beginner. I let you win that hand. This is your house, after all. I didn't want to insult my host."

"What do you mean, you're not a beginner?" Keith asked.

"I've been playing cards with my dad since I was about three."

"Is your dad any good?" Keith asked.

"He'd better be by now," Sally said. "He plays every day all the way from Grand Central Station to Hillcrest. What we have for dessert depends on whether he wins or loses."

"Does he play on the way in, too?" Katia asked.

"Nah," Sally said. "That's when he reads *The Wall Street Journal.*"

Keith sat up straighter as Ian dealt the next hand. Now that he knew Sally really did know how to play, he'd have to pay more attention to the game. Keith played carefully for the next few hands and won them both. Sally won the next one, and Keith was just beginning to get depressed when Lady Luck visited him once again. He drew a pair of kings, put down three cards, drew, and came up with another king. Three kings. That was hard to beat. Nobody did.

"Good hand," Sally said.

Keith scooped the pile of coins and bills toward him with a big grin. Beating some real competition made winning much sweeter.

It was a little before ten when Ian announced, "I'm outta here."

"Just one more hand," Keith said automatically.

"Can't," Ian said. "I've got to go."

Keith stared at the pile of coins in front of him. He was up three dollars for the night, but he knew Sally had won more.

"Don't leave yet," Keith begged Ian. "It's early."

But Sally was already on her feet. "Thanks for the game," she said.

"We should play again," Keith said.

Sally shrugged. "I'm not really into it. I guess I've played with my dad too much."

"You're lucky," Keith said. "I'd love to play with your dad."

"No problem," John put in. "Next time you're on the five thirty-four out of Grand Central, look for the man in the gray suit. You can't miss him," he joked.

"Actually," Sally said, "you don't have to go to New York for the honor. Dad plays with a bunch of Hillcrest geezers once a week."

Keith felt a rush of excitement. "Could you get me into the game?"

"Are you crazy?" Katia interrupted. "You can't play with grown men."

"Why not?" Keith shot back.

"Because they have *real* money they earn at their grown-up jobs," Katia said.

Keith shot her a withering look. "Would you please mind your own business?"

"The stakes are probably higher than you're used to," Sally told him on the way to the front door.

"No problem," Keith said confidently. "If you can get me in, I'm definitely interested."

"I'll ask my dad," Sally said with a shrug.

Katia held her tongue until Keith's friends had left. Then she turned on him. "What are you thinking? You don't have enough money to play with Sally's dad."

"I have enough to get in," Keith told her.

"But what if you lose?"

"Don't worry," Keith told her. "I'm not going to lose."

Katia shook her head. "Good plan, big brother."

Twelve

Wednesday after school Luke decided it was time to take care of an errand he'd been putting off for almost a week. On his way home, he turned into the driveway of a seedy apartment building down the street from his own. The peeling door of a ground-floor apartment sported a sign that read Office.

"This must be it," Luke mumbled to himself. He took a deep breath and knocked on the door.

"Come in," a voice called from inside.

Luke opened the door and walked in. The apartment was empty except for a couple of cheap metal desks that were cluttered with papers. A hulking man in a black polo shirt was talking on the telephone. "Listen, I've gotta call you back," the man grunted into the phone. "I've got a visitor." He replaced the receiver and turned to Luke. "What can I do for you?"

"Um—hi," Luke said, trying to force down his nervousness. "My name is Luke Martinson. I'm Marie Martinson's son."

"Martinson," the man repeated. "You live in the other complex, right?"

"Right," Luke said. "In apartment twelve."

"I suppose you're here because your mother hasn't paid the rent yet," the man said.

"That's right," Luke said, fiddling with the money in his pocket. "She qu—um, lost her job. We've kind of had a hard time coming up with the money."

The landlord studied him. "If you don't mind my saying so, you seem a bit young to be handling the family finances. Why didn't your mom come to see me herself?"

"Because she's busy looking for work," Luke said quickly. He pulled the forty dollars out of his pocket. "She asked me to give this to you. We'll bring the rest by as soon as we have it."

The landlord counted the money and gave Luke a long look. "Listen, kid, I don't know what's going on with your mother. But you have to know forty bucks doesn't come close to covering the rent. What do you want me to do with this?"

"Just take it," Luke said desperately. "I'll bring you more as soon as I can get it."

"Okay, I'll take your measly forty bucks," the landlord said, placing the money in his drawer. "But I want you to tell your mother I'm doing this as a favor. I'm a nice guy, and I don't like evicting drunks—or their kids—but eventually a man's gotta do what a man's gotta do. You know what I mean?"

Luke was burning with humiliation. "I'll tell her," he said quietly. The question was, would she listen?

"I can't believe how warm it is," Suzanne said to Nikki late Saturday morning.

"It's pretty strange for this late in September," Nikki agreed. "Daddy wanted to have the pool closed up last week, but Mom talked him out of it."

Suzanne sat at the side of the pool, kicking her feet in the clear, cool water. "I'm glad she did. It's heaven today."

"Mmm-hmm," Nikki said, sounding sleepy.

Suzanne glanced over her shoulder. Nikki was lying on a lounge chair, soaking up the sun. With her golden hair and pink bikini, Nikki looked as though she belonged in California, not Connecticut. Suzanne envied her. She had never been good at just lying in the sun. She got bored too fast. Even at the beach, she was always tossing a Frisbee or searching for shells. "Your father is a TV producer, right?" Suzanne asked Nikki, breaking the silence.

"Yeah," Nikki said. "He isn't around much. Victoria used to tease me by saying she thought he didn't really exist. At least, I *think* she was kidding."

"You never can tell with Victoria. At least, I can't."

"His new show is a big hit," Nikki went on. "The biggest he's ever had. So now he's working more than ever. I feel like he's a stranger."

"That's too bad," Suzanne said. "You should ask him to spend more time with you."

"I've tried," Nikki said, sitting up. She didn't look sleepy anymore. "But whenever I complain, Mom reminds me that I wouldn't have things like this pool if they didn't work so hard."

"My mom's been working constantly, too," Suzanne commiserated. "Of course, that's nothing new."

Nikki swung her feet off her chair and sat up. "I'm going to get a soda. Want something?"

"Sure. Need help?"

"No," Nikki said, getting to her feet. "You'd better not come in. Mom's getting a facial, and she'd freak if anyone saw her like that."

Suzanne laughed as Nikki padded into the house.

Suzanne pulled her legs out of the pool, then went over and sat on one of the other lounge chairs. She enjoyed the quiet until a surprise visitor interrupted the solitude. Victoria came around the side of the house, her hair damp, wearing a sapphire bikini top and a pair of cutoffs.

"Hey," Victoria said as she walked over to a lounge chair, slipped off her shorts, and made herself comfortable. She reached over and helped herself to some of Suzanne's sunscreen. "Where's Nikki?"

"In the house," Suzanne said, feeling her mood take a nosedive. Spending time with Victoria was a lot of fun for her—right up there with sliding bamboo splinters under her fingernails. "She'll be out in a second."

"I just came from Willis Workout," Victoria said after an uncomfortable silence. "It's my new favorite spot."

Suzanne was more than a little surprised Victoria had anything nice to say to her. "Thanks. Mom's really working hard to make the place perfect. I was just telling Nikki I haven't seen much of her lately."

"Well, she's accomplished a lot. In fact, I'd say she's accomplished the impossible."

"What do you mean?" Suzanne asked, sitting up now to hear what Victoria was about to say.

"Well, Nikki told me that back in glamorous New York you used to work the breakfast shift at some greasy spoon."

Suzanne clenched her hands into fists. "It's called Mona's. So what's your point?"

"Well, I was wondering why you'd want to be a waitress. Did you get credit at school? Did you have a crush on the short-order cook?"

"I did it because we needed the money," Suzanne said, forcing herself not to sound ashamed.

"The money?" Victoria scoffed. "Minimum wage and tips, right?"

"Pretty much." Suzanne was beginning to

lose her patience. "What does Mona's have to do with Willis Workout?"

"I was just wondering how a girl who had to pour coffee for tips can have a mother who can afford a multimillion-dollar piece of real estate," Victoria said.

Multimillion? Suzanne repeated to herself. She knew Willis Workout was fancy, but multimillion-dollar . . .

"What happened?" Victoria went on. "Did you rob a bank or something? Is that why you left Brooklyn?"

Suzanne couldn't think of a reply.

Nikki wandered back toward the pool, carrying two sweating cans of cola. "Victoria! I didn't know you were coming over," she said, saving Suzanne from further interrogation.

"I came to collect on our bet," Victoria said, turning to face Nikki. "I want to wear my new leather jacket on my date with Ian tonight."

Nikki handed a can to Suzanne and then sat down with a sigh. "Well, I guess you won it fair and square. I still can't believe you have a date with Mr. Hard-to-Get. What are you guys doing tonight?"

While the other girls talked, Suzanne stared at the unopened can in her hand. She couldn't stop thinking about Victoria's disturbing words. They reminded her of all the questions she'd managed to forget for weeks. How *had* her mother gotten the money for Willis Workout?

And the house, the car? A few months earlier they'd barely had enough money for Chinese takeout.

Suzanne's mother had said she was in debt. But banks don't give loans to people who don't own anything, Suzanne thought now. You have to promise to turn over your house or something if you can't make the payments. Her mother didn't own anything to turn over—they'd been living in her grandparents' apartment.

An image of her mother wearing a ski mask and holding a gun flitted through Suzanne's mind. Of course, that was ridiculous. Her mother would never rob a bank. But what if she had done something illegal to get the money? What if she'd borrowed it from a loan shark? No! That was crazy, too. Although, Suzanne admitted to herself, her mother had been acting very secretive lately. She was definitely hiding something. . . .

Suzanne's attention was drawn back to the other girls' conversation at the mention of Luke's name.

"A double date sounds cool," Victoria was saying. "But I haven't seen Luke around much lately. What's up with him?"

Nikki sighed, sipping from her can of cola. "He's working a lot. And we had a huge fight last night."

"About what?" Suzanne asked.

"It's so stupid," Nikki said. "Luke freaked

when he saw me wearing a new outfit. He asked me how much it cost, and I told him I didn't know. That just made him crazier. He thinks I spend too much money on clothes."

"As if that's his business," Victoria said.

Nikki shrugged, putting down the can. "The last few times we've gotten together, it's been a total drag. All he wants to do is hang around and play depressing songs on his guitar. I'd like to go on a real date once in a while."

"Trouble in paradise?" Victoria asked.

"Sometimes I just can't deal with all of his dark clouds, you know?" Nikki said.

"Yeah," Victoria said.

Suzanne didn't say anything. She was dying to deal with Luke's problems, just as long as the rest of him was part of the package. Stop it—Luke is Nikki's boyfriend, Suzanne sternly reminded herself. Still, she couldn't help daydreaming about him.

"Brr," Nikki said. "It's getting windy out here."

Suzanne glanced at the sky. A bank of heavy clouds had blocked out the sun.

"It's supposed to rain," Victoria announced. "I heard it on the radio on my way over here."

"So much for the nice weather," Nikki said. The girls stood up and gathered their stuff. "Hey, do either of you want to watch football practice later? Katia and I are going."

Victoria wrinkled her nose. "I get enough of school during the week. I don't need to go on Saturday."

"I have to pass, too," Suzanne said. "I want to spend some time with my mom tonight."

Victoria smirked, but Suzanne ignored her.

Suzanne said good-bye and headed toward her bike. She hated to admit it, but Victoria understood her perfectly. She was going to get the truth out of her mother that night—even if it killed her.

Thirteen

"Thank you," Luke said, smiling. He was standing behind the counter at the Tunesmith. "Come again."

"Thank *you*," the woman said as she took her purchase and headed toward the door. "Bye, now."

When the customer left the store, Luke's smile faded. He slipped the twenty she had given him into his pocket, closed the register, and put the register key into his pocket, jamming it against the wad of bills he'd already pocketed.

Luke had taken a "loan" from the Tunesmith every shift he'd worked since he'd met with the landlord a few days earlier. So far he'd taken more than a hundred bucks. He expected to be caught and fired any second, but Rick hadn't so much as given him one suspicious look. Luke imagined that Rick was too busy zooming around the lake on his new boat to notice his profits had dropped by a few dollars a day—or at least every day Luke had worked.

Pulling a battered copy of *Rolling Stone* out from under the counter, Luke flipped through the pages. He was supposed to be helping Mark shelve disks, but he didn't feel like it. He was exhausted.

Luke hadn't been sleeping much. His mother had been out until dawn almost every night that week. Luke had just lain in bed, worrying what would happen to him if his mother didn't pull it together.

"Yo," Mark called. "Look lively."

Luke glanced up in time to see Rick stroll in the door. The boss was in his early thirties, and that day he was wearing chinos with a sharp crease, boat shoes, and a navy blue windbreaker. His close-cropped brown hair had a bit of gray at the temples.

"Hi, boss," Mark said, organizing a group of misplaced CDs.

"The shelves are looking good," Rick greeted him as he headed toward the counter.

Feeling guilty, Luke closed the magazine and quickly put the register key in the drawer beneath the counter. "Hey, Rick," he said.

"Hi, Luke." Rick stopped in front of him.

Luke couldn't read Rick's face. He looked troubled. Or maybe annoyed. Angry?

"What's up?" Rick asked.

"Nothing much," Luke said. "I was just about to start shelving some disks."

Rick studied Luke. He seemed to be considering something.

Luke was suddenly having a hard time breathing. The moment he'd been dreading had arrived. Rick was about to confront him about the missing money.

"The shelving can wait," Rick finally said. "I want to talk to you in the office."

Wordlessly Luke followed Rick toward the back of the store, a thousand excuses and denials swimming in his head.

Rick shut the office door behind them. "Sit down," he told Luke.

Luke sank into a chair.

Rick leaned against the front of the desk, facing Luke. He picked up a stapler and started to turn it over and over.

Luke watched with a feeling of dread. Rick seemed pretty nervous. But not nearly as nervous as Luke was feeling.

"I'm not sure how to say this," Rick said carefully. "But I've noticed something lately."

"Noticed?" Luke's voice squeaked.

Rick nodded. "You've been working practically every afternoon."

"You said it was okay if I took some extra shifts," Luke said. "And Adele wanted to drop some hours."

"I know," Rick said. "But you look exhausted.

149

I think you should ease off. Take fewer shifts."

Luke was confused. This conversation wasn't going the way he'd imagined. What was Rick getting at? "I can't. I need the money."

"Oh," Rick said. "Well . . . Then I'm going to give you a raise. Say a buck an hour. That way you can take one more afternoon off each week and still make about the same amount."

"You don't have to do that," Luke said, beginning to relax.

"I know." Rick set down the stapler and met Luke's eyes. "But I want to. You've always worked hard for me, and I think you deserve it. In fact, since I'm such a nice guy, I'm going to give you the rest of the afternoon off."

"What?" Luke asked.

"The customers love it when I'm here. Besides, the weather is crappy," Rick went on, moving toward the door of his office. "Since I can't be out on the lake, I might as well shelve some CDs. Get out of here before I change my mind. Go take a nap."

Luke stood up and followed Rick to the door. "Listen, Rick," he said awkwardly. "I really appreciate this. Thanks. Really."

Rick patted him on the back. "You're welcome. But don't tell the other employees what a great guy I am. I couldn't take the pressure of being nice to everyone."

"No problem," Luke said numbly.

A minute later Luke was standing on Main

Street, feeling unsure of what to do next. He wasn't in any hurry to get home, that was for sure. His mother was probably still sleeping off the previous night's binge. But Luke had to go *somewhere*. The sky was filled with clouds that looked as if they planned to hang around for a while. It was drizzling, and a cold wind was kicking up. Luke was shivering in his T-shirt.

He stopped for a moment and pulled the money out of his pocket. Fifty-two bucks. He wondered if it would be enough to get the landlord to mellow out. Probably not.

Fifty-two bucks that belonged to Rick, the guy who was worried Luke wasn't getting enough sleep. Tears pricked at Luke's eyes. Somehow he'd become a criminal.

It's not my fault my mother's a drunk, Luke told himself. He was just coping as best he could, doing what he had to do to survive. But deep down Luke couldn't allow himself to believe that. He knew he could have turned to his friends for help or gone to a counselor at school. Stealing from Rick wasn't the only way out; it was just the easiest. This way he didn't have to admit to Nikki that he was poor and helpless. But hadn't he told his mother that Nikki didn't care about things like that?

Suddenly Luke knew what he wanted to do with his unexpected freedom. He wanted to wrap his arms around Nikki and lose himself in her kisses. And then he wanted to tell her about what had been going on at home. For a second Luke felt a flicker of doubt. He'd never given Nikki the chance to listen before—she didn't want to hear about his major problems, he'd told himself over and over. But she had to listen now. If Nikki really loved him, she'd know how important this was.

Luke ducked into a phone booth. It wasn't a real booth with full-length glass sides, the kind that would protect him from the wind, but more of a phone on a stick. He dropped a quarter into the slot and punched in Nikki's number.

"Stewart residence," came a voice. It was Rita, the Stewarts' maid.

"Rita? It's Luke. Is Nikki there?"

"No, she went out. I'll tell her you called."

"Thanks." He hung up, disappointed. Where could Nikki be?

Luke picked up the phone and called information. He got Victoria's number and dialed it. "Hey, Luke," she said when she came to the phone. "Long time no see. Where've you been hiding yourself?"

"The Tunesmith, mostly," Luke told her, holding the phone between his ear and neck. He put his hands into his jeans pockets to keep them warm. "Listen, I'm looking for Nikki. Rita said she wasn't home, and I thought she might be over there."

"No, but I know where she is. She went to watch football practice with Katia."

"Why didn't you go?" Luke asked.

"In the rain?" Victoria said. "What's the point? I'm not interested in any of the guys on the team."

Luke had to laugh at Victoria's bluntness. "Okay, well, thanks. I'll look for her on the field."

"Later."

Luke hung up and walked briskly toward Hillcrest High. Halfway there, he decided it hadn't been such a bright idea. It wasn't raining hard, but his T-shirt was already soaked though and his arms were cold. Boy, the weather sure is strange today, he thought. Still, Luke kept walking. He had to see Nikki.

As Luke approached the football field he spotted her on the sidelines, talking to one of the players. The player's uniform was covered with mud. He was holding his helmet in one hand.

The other players were packing up their gear or jogging toward the locker room. There was no sign of Katia.

Luke watched Nikki touch the guy's arm. He heard her laugh. What's going on here? Luke wondered, walking faster. Moving closer, he realized Nikki wasn't talking to just any guy—it was Keith. Luke felt a sting of annoyance. His best friend was being awfully chummy with his girlfriend.

"Hey," Luke yelled, hurrying toward them.

Nikki jumped at the sound of his voice and quickly dropped her hand from Keith's arm. "Luke! I thought you were working."

153

Luke thought Keith looked guilty. "Hi," Keith said.

"What's up?" Luke replied.

"Practice just ended," Keith said. "Nikki and I were thinking about going bowling."

Nikki nodded eagerly. "Want to come?"

"Since when are you guys into bowling?" Luke's question came out sounding nastier than he'd planned. What he wanted to ask was, Since when have you guys been such great friends? A part of Luke knew he was overreacting. After all, Nikki and Keith had invited him to come with them. But a more suspicious part of him pointed out that it was only because he had appeared unexpectedly.

"We aren't," Nikki said, laughing. "Bowling is so geeky. That's why it'll be a total riot."

"Yeah, a riot." Luke tried to push down his anger and disappointment, but he couldn't help feeling sorry for himself. He'd been working so much lately, he'd barely seen Nikki the entire week. He needed some time alone with her. Cracking up over gutter balls wasn't exactly what he had in mind. Besides, he felt as if he was crashing Nikki and Keith's party.

"So, what do you say?" Nikki asked, touching Luke's cold, damp arm.

"You guys go ahead," Luke decided. "I'm not in the mood."

A flicker of concern passed over Nikki's face. "Are you sure?"

"Yeah, yeah, I'm sure," Luke said, taking a step away.

"Well, okay." Keith shrugged. "Do you at least want a ride home?"

"No." Luke's anger was growing. His so-called friends sure had accepted his refusal quickly—almost as if they didn't really want him to come. There was no way he was getting into a car with them now. "I'd rather walk."

"Give me a call later," Keith said uneasily.

Luke gave Nikki a long look. Then he walked away, unsure of where he was going. As he walked Luke wondered why the two people he loved most in the world couldn't sense the pain he was feeling.

Fourteen

Late Saturday afternoon Suzanne climbed on her bike and steered it toward Willis Workout. She had spent most of the afternoon at home, thinking about her mother. By five o'clock she couldn't wait any longer. She put on her waterproof jacket and rode through the light rain.

As Suzanne pedaled down the road a minivan passed, splashing her with muddy water. Suzanne groaned. The New York City subway might be a pain sometimes, but at least it was dry.

Suzanne was relieved to turn into the Willis Workout parking lot. As she pulled in, a black limousine was pulling out. Suzanne couldn't see through the limousine's tinted windows, but it looked as if her mother had a rich new customer. A rock star, maybe.

Suzanne coasted up to the bike rack in front of the club, locked her bike, and hurried inside. The rain seemed to be coming down harder by the minute. She called hello to Tim as she grabbed a towel from behind the desk to dry off. Tim told her she could find her mother in the large studio. Suzanne was relieved to discover there was no class going on. Her mother was stacking mats.

"Hi, honey," her mother greeted her. "You're soaked."

"I know," she said. "It was just drizzling when I left the house, but now it's pouring outside." Suzanne paused for a moment, unsure of how to ask her mother what she wanted to know. "Hey—who just left in the limo?"

"Limo?" her mother asked in a strained voice. "I don't know."

Suzanne's heart pounded at her mother's bad attempt at a lie. Maybe the passenger of that limousine had something to do with her strange behavior.

"Stop lying to me, Mom," Suzanne pleaded. Finished with the towel, she tossed it over her shoulder. "I want to know what's going on!"

"Keep your voice down," her mother scolded.

"Fine," Suzanne said. "Just tell me."

"Nothing is going on."

"I don't believe you!" Suzanne said, losing her patience. "I know you're keeping a secret from me. You've been acting strange ever since we left Brooklyn."

"I think your imagination is running away with you," her mother said.

"No, it's not," Suzanne said, trying to sound calm and reasonable. "The kids at school say this place cost millions of dollars—"

"Not millions," Ms. Willis said with a little laugh.

"Okay," Suzanne said. "One million. I still don't understand how you're doing it. And what were Grammy and Pops so mad about when we moved away? What are you hiding from me?"

"I think it's better if you don't know," Ms. Willis said.

"So you *are* hiding something!"

"I didn't say that."

"You did so! Come on, I want to know the truth. Did you borrow the money from a loan shark?" Suzanne's eyes widened. "Is that who was in the limousine? You didn't miss a payment, did you?"

"Suzanne!" her mother said. "Get a grip. I didn't borrow the money from a loan shark. That's ridiculous. It's nothing sinister like that. It's just that I have a—silent partner. Grammy and Pops don't approve of my taking money from him."

"Who is it?" Suzanne demanded immediately. "It's that S person, isn't it? The one who sent the roses."

Her mother laughed and shook her head. "You don't miss a thing, do you?"

"Does that mean I'm right?" Suzanne demanded, hands on her hips.

Wearily, her mother nodded.

"What's his real name?" Suzanne asked. "Where did you meet him?"

"Sorry," her mother said. "But I'm not answering any more questions."

"Mom, I have a right to know."

"I'm afraid I don't agree," her mother said. She stopped stacking mats and faced Suzanne. "My partner wants to remain anonymous, and I plan to respect that. That's why he's a *silent* partner."

"Is he some kind of criminal?"

"No," her mother said firmly. "Let's drop this, okay? In fact, I don't want you to mention my partner to any of your friends. Just let them think Willis Workout is some kind of financial miracle."

Suzanne didn't answer.

Her mother came toward her, arms out. "Let's not fight, sweetie. Things are going so well. Willis Workout is a success, you're happy at your new school—everything is perfect."

"Fine," Suzanne whispered as her mother hugged her.

Ms. Willis let go and went back to straightening up.

Regardless of what she said, Suzanne wasn't about to let her mother off the hook. She planned to get the whole story out of her as soon as possible. The trick was not to let her mother know she was pumping her for information. Sooner or later she'd let something slip.

"So, what do you want to do tonight?"

Suzanne forced her voice to be light. "Let's rent a video and make chocolate-chip cookies."

"Oh, honey, I'm sorry," her mother said. "But I can't. Didn't I tell you? I have a date with Bob Houghton tonight. He's picking me up any minute."

"He's picking you up here?" Suzanne asked.

Her mother nodded.

Suzanne groaned. "I was hoping for a ride home. It's pouring, remember?"

"Well, I'm sure Bob won't mind driving you home," Ms. Willis said.

"Mr. Houghton?" Suzanne asked. "No, I don't want to do that. I'd feel like I was crashing your date."

"It's not a big deal," Ms. Willis said.

"Forget about it," Suzanne said firmly.

"Then I guess it's pedal power for you," Ms. Willis said. "Why don't you hang out here for a while? The rain should stop soon."

Suzanne sighed. "I think I'll just go home now," she decided.

"Okay, honey." Her mother gave her a kiss. "Be careful. And don't forget to lock the door when you're in the house. There's plenty of stuff in the fridge for your dinner. I'll be home early."

"Okay." Suzanne headed for the door, feeling confused and angry. She had hoped her mother would put her fears to rest, but she was more confused than ever. And she wasn't looking forward to spending Saturday night alone. When she got outside, she was pleased to see that at least the rain had stopped. A blanket of clouds still hung low in the sky, but a few rays of evening sunshine were peeking through.

Suzanne unlocked her bike, climbed on, and started the trip into Hillcrest. As she rode she thought back on her conversation with her mother. Why would her mother's partner want to be silent? It sounded fishy to Suzanne. She couldn't shake the feeling that her mother had done something awful to get the money.

Suzanne got off her bike to carry it up the stairs of the footbridge that crossed the train tracks. A few seconds later she was coasting down Main Street. As she passed Town Hall she spotted Luke sitting on one of the benches in front of the impressive building, looking cold and miserable. Suzanne sensed something was wrong. Luke didn't seem to be waiting for anyone, and he looked awfully sad.

Suzanne put her head down and started to pedal faster. She hadn't spoken to Luke since he'd attacked her at lunch the other day. His words still stung. Suzanne had already ridden by when Luke called out to her.

"Getting some exercise?"

She braked to a stop. "Are you talking to me?" she asked with an attitude.

The weak smile Luke was wearing faded. "Well, excuse me. Sorry I bothered," he said.

Furious, Suzanne pushed off. But then she changed her mind, backed the bike up so that she was in front of Luke, and planted her feet. "I don't know why you hate me so much," she said, glaring at Luke. "I've never done one bad thing to you. I guess you're just another spoiled brat."

"Yeah, right. As if I had even a penny to my name!" Luke jumped to his feet.

Suzanne stared at him for a moment, then started to ride away.

"Fine!" Luke called after her. "Run home to Daddy!"

With that comment Suzanne snapped. She stopped her bike again, dropped it, and marched back to Luke. "Who do you think you are? What gives you the right to stand there and judge me? You don't know the first thing about me."

"Why don't you tell me something, then?" Luke challenged her.

"Fine," Suzanne said. "First of all, I'm not on my way home to Daddy. He's dead!"

Suzanne watched as all of the anger drained out of Luke's face. He slumped back down on the bench. "I'm sorry. I shouldn't have said that."

"Forget it." Suzanne's voice was tight. "He's been gone a long time. I'm over it."

"No, you're not," Luke said.

"How would you know?"

"My father's dead, too," Luke said. "He's been gone nine years, and I'm still not over it."

Suzanne considered this information for a long moment. "How did he die?" she asked softly.

"Cancer," Luke said. "I was seven when we found out. He died the next year."

"Oh, man, that's rough," Suzanne whispered. She joined him on the bench.

"What happened to your dad?" Luke asked.

"He died in a car accident before I was born," Suzanne told him.

"Maybe it's better that way," Luke said. "Since you never met him, you can't miss him that much."

Suzanne shook her head. "I'd give anything to have met him just once." For a minute Suzanne was lost in her thoughts. Then she shook her head and told Luke, "I'd better get going."

Luke reached out and touched her arm. "Suzanne, I'm sorry I've been so mean to you."

"Forget it," Suzanne said, still sitting on the bench.

"I haven't been myself lately." Luke laughed bitterly. "Not for a long time, actually."

"Are you okay?" Suzanne asked. "You really looked down in the dumps when I rode up."

"Yeah, you're right. I was—I am."

"How come?"

"Oh, it's my mom. . . ."

Suzanne laughed. "You too? We really do have a lot in common."

"Why?" Luke asked with a shy grin. "What's up with your mom?"

With a sigh, Suzanne moved closer to Luke. She hadn't told anybody how worried she was about her mother. Why should she tell Luke? She hardly even knew him.

"She's not sick, is she?" Luke asked gently.

Suzanne shook her head rapidly. She knew it would feel good to share her secret. Maybe she *should* tell Luke. Maybe the fact that he'd asked was reason enough. "I'm really worried about her," she said carefully. "Maybe it's nothing, but she won't tell me where she got the money to open Willis Workout."

"Have you seen her do anything wrong?" Luke asked.

"I just have suspicions."

"Forget about them," Luke said firmly.

Suzanne's eyes widened. How could he dismiss her problems like that? Especially when she'd just decided he was a nice guy. "What do you mean?" she demanded.

"Look at it this way," Luke said. "Has your mother ever accused you of doing something you didn't really do?"

"Of course," Suzanne said. "She *is* my mother."

"You hate it, don't you?" Luke asked.

"Absolutely."

"Why?"

"Because she should trust me."

"And you should trust *her*," Luke said.

Suzanne didn't say anything for a moment. Then she shook her head and laughed. "Know what? You're right."

Luke nodded without smiling.

"So what about you?" Suzanne asked. "What's up with your mom?"

Luke was silent for a moment. Then he said, "Well, we've been having a few disagreements about curfews."

"Tell me about it," Suzanne said. "My mom goes ballistic when I miss mine."

"I'm sure it'll blow over," Luke said. "Anyway . . . I guess I'd better get going."

Suzanne glanced at her watch. It was a little past six o'clock. "Wow, you really do have an early curfew," she joked.

Luke smiled weakly and stood up. "I told you my mother was driving me insane."

"So, what are you doing tonight? Are you going out with Nikki?"

"Just going home to work on some songs," Luke said.

"Can I come?" Suzanne couldn't believe she'd been brave enough to ask, and she immediately regretted her boldness. Luke looked extremely uncomfortable.

"I—I'm sorry," she mumbled. "I shouldn't— Listen, I'll see you at school."

"Wait," Luke said softly. "You don't understand. It's not that I don't want to spend time with you. It's just that I—"

Suzanne was expecting him to say, "I already have a girlfriend, remember?"

"I can't have you to my place," Luke finished.

When Suzanne saw how miserable he looked,

she forgot her embarrassment. She wondered if something serious was going on at Luke's house.

"Listen, why don't you go home, grab your guitar, and come over to my house?" Suzanne offered.

"I have a better idea."

"You do?" Suzanne said.

"Yeah," Luke said. "The Hillcrest Country Club is my favorite place. After hours, you can sneak onto the golf course."

"The golf course?"

"It's really beautiful there," Luke said.

"Well, it sounds different," Suzanne admitted. "Would it be okay if I brought a picnic? I haven't had dinner yet."

"Sounds great," Luke said. "I'm starving. I'll walk over to your house and pick you up in about an hour."

"Perfect," Suzanne said.

As Suzanne watched Luke walk away she wondered why Nikki wasn't with him. She was glad he wanted to hang out with her, though. They both needed a friend to lean on.

Fifteen

"No—don't go that way!" Nikki yelled, jumping up and down. "More to the left, the *left!*"

Keith groaned as Nikki's bowling ball rolled into the gutter on the right side of the lane.

"I missed that one on purpose," Nikki told him lightly. "I didn't want to beat you by *too* much."

"Thanks," Keith said, sitting at the scoring table. "I don't know where I'd be without your pity."

"You're welcome," Nikki said, waltzing over to join him. "But don't get used to it. Next game I'm going to be merciless."

"You're so kind," Keith joked.

"Sorry," Nikki said. "But I've got to get some practice in before I join the pro tour."

Keith nodded as if there was no arguing with that.

Nikki giggled. In truth, Keith's score was about twice as good as hers. Still, she wasn't half as bad a bowler as she had thought she would be. So what if one of her balls had jumped over into the next lane? It had struck down a couple of pins there, hadn't it? And besides, she was improving with every game.

"Having fun?" Keith asked.

"Definitely," Nikki said. "I'm so glad I thought of this."

"*I* thought of this," Keith said.

Nikki waved her hand as if to say it didn't matter. "Details, details."

Keith threw down the pencil he had used to mark down Nikki's score and got up to take his turn. Nikki couldn't help smiling. Being out with Keith was so different from being out with Luke. She had so much fun with Keith . . . he really knew how to make her laugh.

Everything with Luke was so deadly serious all the time. Sometimes when she tried to joke with Luke, he didn't realize she wasn't being serious. He'd start to make some thoughtful response to her inane comment. Nikki didn't understand why, but some of the same things that had attracted her to Luke in the first place were starting to drive her crazy.

"Earth to Nikki," Keith said, walking back to the table. "It's your turn, space cadet."

"Oops, sorry." Nikki stepped up to the ball return and slid her fingers into the hot pink ball she'd chosen. Supporting the ball with two hands, she stood at the end of the lane. She took a deep breath and concentrated, then slowly took five steps forward, smoothly bringing the ball back at the same time. She brought her arm forward and carefully released the ball. She was surprised to see it rolling straight down the lane at a good speed.

"Looking good," Keith called out.

Nikki held her breath until the ball crashed right into the lead pin. Seven of the pins fell immediately. Another teetered back and forth, side to side—and then finally fell over. Two pins were left standing.

"Ooh, so close," Nikki said.

Keith had come up behind her. "You're in good shape," he said seriously. "The two standing pins are close together. You have a chance to get them with your second ball."

"Get real," Nikki said. "They're way over to the side. If I aim for them, my ball will go in the gutter."

"Do you want me to help you?" Keith asked, standing now.

"Sure," Nikki said.

When the pink ball popped up in the ball return, Nikki picked it up. She stood on the spot Keith had pointed out. Keith stood close behind her. Without taking any steps, Keith guided her arm back and forth.

"Now," he whispered in her ear when it was time to release the ball. The second the ball left her hand, Nikki became aware of Keith. He was standing so close to her, she could feel the warmth of his body. She felt a delicious tingle run across her skin as she watched the ball roll down the lane. To her amazement, the ball squarely hit one of the pins, knocking both to the ground.

"That was so cool!" Nikki turned to face Keith and threw her arms around him. Before she knew what was happening, he'd wrapped his arms around her waist and pulled her closer. Nikki could feel the strength in his arms, in his chest.

Nikki cleared her throat and gently pulled away. "That was fantastic," she said, trying to keep her voice light. "I must be beating you by more than ever now."

"We make a good team," Keith said in a husky voice.

"We do," Nikki agreed. "But next time I want to do it by myself."

"Are you sure?" Keith asked. "It's more fun when I help."

Nikki gave him a sly smile. "I think I'd better not answer that."

"Probably not," he admitted.

Nikki noticed that Keith seemed nervous as he picked up his ball. He didn't look at her or make any jokes as he sent it rolling down the lane. Nikki couldn't ignore the fact that the atmosphere had become charged. Her body was tuned in to Keith's every move. The game didn't seem important anymore. And Nikki didn't feel like laughing.

Should I say something? Nikki wondered. After all, she and Keith had been friends for years. She didn't want one innocent hug to come between them.

"Hey, Keith," she started.

But Keith was watching the ball. It hit the pins strongly, and they all fell. "Strike!" Keith yelled. With a whoop, he swooped Nikki up and spun her around.

"Congratulations!"

Keith stopped turning and slowly let Nikki slide to the ground.

Nikki's heart was pounding. There was no denying that Keith was having an effect on her. She hugged him closer.

He looked into her eyes, seriously and with longing. He stroked the side of her face.

Nikki closed her eyes. She could feel Keith's warm breath on her face. But just as their lips were about to meet, Keith pulled back.

"I—I can't do this," he said.

"Is it because of Luke?" she asked.

Suddenly Keith looked angry. "Yes, it's because of Luke! He's still your boyfriend, isn't he?"

Nikki sighed. "Yes, but it's just— I don't know. He's been in such a bad mood lately."

"Is that the only reason you were about to kiss me?" Keith asked. "Because Luke's been in a bad mood?"

"No," Nikki said, touching his arm. "Well, maybe. Oh, I don't know!"

"Did he tell you what happened?" Keith asked quietly.

"What do you mean?" Nikki demanded.

"His mom quit her latest job," Keith said. "That's why he's been so down lately."

Nikki's jaw dropped. "You're kidding! Why didn't he tell me? Why didn't *you* tell me?"

Keith shrugged.

"We've got to find him," Nikki said decisively, picking up her bag and jacket.

"Now?" Keith asked.

"Now," Nikki said.

"What about the game?"

"Forget the game. Let's go."

"Fine," Keith agreed. He picked up his jacket, but then he paused.

"What's the matter?" she asked impatiently. "Let's go!"

"It's nothing."

"C'mon, what's up?"

"Sometimes I wish I were Luke, money problems and all."

"Why would you want that?" Nikki asked.

"Because I'd also have you."

Suzanne ducked under a tree branch. "Wow, this is amazing," she said, standing on the golf course at the Hillcrest Country Club. A flag waved on the putting green nearby. "Is this grass real?" The grass was perfectly regular, very closely cut, and intensely green.

"Sort of," Luke said. "I mean, it would never grow this way on its own. I think the country club has about eight men who work on the greens full time."

"You'd think they'd have guard dogs or something," Suzanne said as she gingerly took a few steps out from the trees. "Haven't you ever gotten caught? I mean, we are trespassing, aren't we?"

"Technically, yes. But I've been coming here for years, and nobody seems to mind." Luke shrugged. "If you're worried, we can leave."

"No," Suzanne said quickly. She wasn't going to let anything ruin her evening with Luke. She boldly stepped forward and set down the grocery bag she was carrying.

Luke sat down and laid his guitar case next to him. "So, what's for dinner?"

"Everything I could find in the fridge." She opened the bag. "Apples, cheese, bread. A few other things."

"Sounds good to me. Hey, look out, the grass is wet," Luke said, stripping off his jean jacket and sweatshirt. "Here, we can sit on this."

They settled onto the jacket and sweatshirt, and Suzanne arranged the food on the grass in front of them.

"Pasta salad, my favorite," Luke said. "Hey, where are the forks?"

Suzanne covered her mouth with her hand. "You're not going to believe this. . . ."

"You forgot them, didn't you?" Luke brushed

the hair out of his eyes with his fingers. "Well, don't worry. We'll just have to eat with our hands."

Suzanne could only pretend to eat. Luke's presence had completely ruined her appetite, making her heart and her stomach dance around each other. Luke didn't have any problem eating, though. It was as if he hadn't had a decent meal in weeks.

When he finally finished, he lay back and sighed contentedly. "Thanks for the food."

"It was nothing," Suzanne said. "Hey, can you see any stars?"

"Mmm-hmm," Luke murmured, looking into the sky.

Suzanne wondered if she should lie back next to Luke. He hadn't exactly encouraged her.

"Thousands of stars," he said.

Well, that was encouragement, wasn't it? Suzanne lay back. "Wow," she murmured. "There really *are* a lot of stars. I could never see so many in New York."

Luke rolled over on his side so that he was facing Suzanne. "Then I guess it's a good thing you moved here."

Hardly daring to breathe, Suzanne turned toward Luke. "I think it was a very good thing."

Luke didn't smile or laugh or crack a joke. He just stared into Suzanne's eyes.

She couldn't move. Even though they weren't touching, it was a very intimate moment.

"Suzanne," Luke whispered.

"Yes?"

174

Luke closed his eyes and, with what seemed like a great effort, sat up. The spell was destroyed.

"Where are you going?" Suzanne asked without stopping to think.

Luke took a deep breath. "I'm going to introduce you to an old musician's tradition."

Suzanne sat up. "What's that?"

"It's called singing for your supper," Luke said. He opened his guitar case and gently lifted the instrument out. Settling the guitar on his crossed legs, he caressed a few chords out of it. He bent his head over the guitar, his hair falling forward. Suzanne couldn't see his eyes. Slowly the idle strumming developed into a sad melody.

"Suzanne, there's something I have to tell you." Luke let the guitar go quiet as he looked up to meet her gaze.

"I have to tell you something, too."

Luke glanced down. "Let me go first. Before I lose my nerve."

"Okay."

"I can't get you out of my mind," he admitted.

Suzanne sat up but didn't reply.

"I guess that's why I was so mean to you the other day," Luke said. "I'm afraid of you. I'm afraid of how I feel about you."

Suzanne just nodded slowly.

"I guess you don't want to hear this," Luke said harshly.

"You're wrong," she said quickly. "I do want to hear it."

175

Suzanne felt a weird mix of emotions. She was elated that Luke liked her. Guilty that she liked him back. And confused. Did she really want this? Nikki was the best friend she had in Hillcrest. How could Suzanne hurt her?

She took a deep breath and tried to put her feelings into words. "I mean, I understand. Every time I see you, I feel—so many things all at once. Especially . . ." Her voice trailed off.

"Especially what?" Luke gently prompted.

"Especially when I see you with Nikki." There—she'd said it.

"Nikki," Luke repeated softly.

"It's just that I owe her so much," Suzanne said. "We've been so close ever since that night at the concert."

"I owe her a lot, too," Luke said, putting the guitar back into its case. "We've been through some hard times, and we've always stuck together."

Tears pooled in Suzanne's eyes. "Maybe we should just forget about all this," she said in a shaky voice.

For a long moment neither of them spoke. Suzanne thought about what Nikki had said that morning at the pool—that she was having a harder and harder time connecting with Luke. Suzanne felt herself getting angry. Nikki had everything she could ever want, and it seemed she didn't really want Luke. So why shouldn't Suzanne have him? Trembling, she waited to hear what Luke would say next. What was he thinking about?

Luke took a deep breath. "We can't ignore our feelings," he said intensely.

Suzanne's heart soared.

"It would be wrong," Luke went on. "It wouldn't be fair to Nikki. It wouldn't be fair to us."

"What should we do?" Suzanne asked.

"Tell Nikki the truth," Luke said. "It won't be easy, you know."

"It'll be horrible," Suzanne said.

"It's still the right thing to do," Luke said, moving closer to Suzanne.

She moved even closer to him. "When?"

"As soon as possible," Luke said. "Tomorrow morning." He put his arm around her shoulder and pulled her nearer still. But Suzanne felt as if he were far away—perhaps imagining the difficult conversation he was going to have with Nikki.

"I need to talk to her, too," Suzanne said.

Luke nodded, looking serious. Then he slowly turned toward Suzanne. She held her breath as he brought his lips close to hers. They kissed briefly, their eyes open, and then Luke pulled away. After a pause, she leaned over and gave him another tentative kiss.

Then, as if some barrier holding him back had suddenly collapsed, Luke pulled Suzanne into a kiss that was almost painful in its intensity. She slipped her hands around his back and let her worries about Nikki float away.

But then Suzanne felt Luke's arms stiffen, and he jerked back. Suzanne opened her eyes in time to see Luke jump to his feet. He stumbled, and then he was running across the golf course, away from Suzanne.

"Nikki!" she heard him yell. "Wait, please wait!"

Then Suzanne saw Nikki running across the golf course. With a jolt, she realized Nikki must have seen her kissing Luke.

"Leave me alone!" Nikki yelled.

"I have to talk to you! Please, Nikki!"

A moment passed, and Suzanne was left alone on the golf course.

Sixteen

Victoria opened her purse and pulled out her favorite cinnamon-colored lipstick. She moved the rearview mirror so she could see her reflection, smoothed on some lipstick, and fluffed up her hair.

"You're irresistible," she whispered to herself. As she got out of the car and walked up to Ian's house, she imagined her friends' reaction when she told them all about her date with the hardest-to-get guy at Hillcrest High. With a little shiver, she imagined Ian asking her if he could kiss her. One thing was certain—she wasn't going to give in easily. She'd make him beg and grovel first. Victoria laughed softly. She was going to enjoy that.

Victoria was wearing an outfit guaranteed to grab the attention of any guy. Her black skirt showed off her tanned bare legs, and her high heels accentuated her toned calf and thigh muscles. The matching top left her shoulders, back, and stomach exposed. She had thrown her hard-won leather jacket over one shoulder and left her wavy red hair down. Victoria had worn this very outfit—without the jacket—to a dance club in New York, and she'd practically had to beat them off with a stick. It was a little fancy for hanging out in Ian's room, but she wanted him to know how special this date was to her.

Victoria rang the doorbell.

A long time passed before Ian finally opened the door. "Oh. Hi," he said.

"Hello," Victoria purred. Inside she was fuming. Ian sounded as if he'd forgotten she was coming over.

Ian raised one eyebrow as he took in Victoria's outfit. But he didn't say a word. Victoria could have said a lot about *his* appearance, though. The guy was drop-dead gorgeous, but he looked as if he hadn't been out of his room all day. He was wearing sweatpants and a baseball cap, and he needed a shave. Victoria told herself his careless look wasn't necessarily a bad sign. There was something almost intimate about it. It proved he was comfortable with her.

She cleared her throat. "Aren't you going to invite me in?"

Ian stepped aside. "Sure."

Victoria followed Ian into the house. Without a word, without even offering her a drink or making a moment's small talk, he headed up the stairs to his room. "It's past ten now, so we can log on right away."

"Cool," Victoria said, trying to sound enthusiastic as she followed him up the steps.

Ian opened the door to his room.

Victoria stepped in and looked around with curiosity. She was probably the only girl at Hillcrest who had ever been in Ian's bedroom—except for Sally Ross, of course. Victoria planned to remember every detail so she could tell her friends later. The room was pretty much as Victoria had imagined. It was dominated by a huge bookcase overflowing with books. The computer, with an immense color monitor, took up most of Ian's desk.

Ian sat down in a black leather desk chair and began typing on the keyboard.

Victoria looked for another chair to pull up to the desk, but there wasn't one. The only other place to sit was on the bed, which was a good ten feet from the desk. She might as well have sat in Siberia. She walked up to Ian and put a hand on his shoulder. He continued to type.

"You really know your way around that thing, don't you?" Victoria said, searching for something to say.

"Sure," Ian said. He didn't miss a beat as he typed away. "It's not as hard as people think. It just takes a little time."

Time some people would prefer spending with other people, Victoria thought. Or getting dressed like a normal human being.

"Okay, we're in," Ian said.

"I'm so excited," Victoria said, leaning over Ian's shoulder to get a look at the screen. "So this is the Cyberlounge. Cool place."

Ian gave her a strange look.

Victoria had to admit she sounded like an idiot. Lines of text were quickly scrolling by, and she read the screen for a while. Several conversations seemed to be going on at once. One was about a new Loving Lobster CD. Someone else just kept typing "Big Brother is watching you" over and over again. All of the messages were mixed together, which made it difficult to follow any of the conversations.

"Where's this stuff coming from?" Victoria asked.

"Who knows?" Ian said with a shrug, never taking his eyes off the screen. "Probably from all over the country. Of course, one of these people could be right next door."

"Can't you find out?" Victoria asked.

"Not unless the person decides to tell you their real identity," Ian said. "But hardly anyone ever does that. One of the greatest things about communicating online is that nobody knows who you really are."

"But they know your name, don't they?" Victoria asked.

"No." Ian sounded excited for once. "Look at the left side of the screen. See? Everyone uses a handle. You know, like on a CB radio. The handle gives you an idea of how the person wants to be known."

"What's your handle?" Victoria asked, relieved that Ian was at least holding a conversation with her.

Ian didn't answer. "All right!" he exclaimed. "L. Stone is here."

"L. Stone?" Victoria repeated. "That sounds like a real name."

"It is a real name," Ian said. "But it's not *her* real name. Think about it."

Victoria could feel her anger rising. Why did Ian always insist on making her feel so stupid? "You're right, it's obvious," she said. "L. Stone must smoke a lot of pot. Not a very attractive habit if you ask me."

Ian turned and looked at her as if she were out of her mind. "That's not what it means. L. Stone stands for Lucy Stone."

"And who is Lucy Stone?" Victoria asked impatiently. "Fred Flintstone's cousin?"

Ian shook his head. "Lucy Stone was one of the founders of the feminist movement. I'm surprised you don't know that. Especially since you're a girl."

Ha! Victoria thought. So Ian *did* know she was a girl. "Well, I think L. Stone is a stupid handle," Victoria said. "I mean, why would you want to use someone else's name? It's not very creative."

"But it says so much about who she is," Ian argued. "At least to people who know enough to understand its meaning."

Victoria was fuming. She might not have known much about feminist history, but she knew an insult when she heard one. She glared at Ian, but he'd turned his attention back to the computer, his fingers flying over the keyboard. He was having a furious conversation with L. Stone, completely ignoring Victoria.

Victoria grabbed hold of one of his wrists. "Is L. Stone a girl?" she demanded.

Ian glanced up at her. "Yeah. Why?"

Victoria raised an eyebrow. "How can you be so sure?" she asked archly. "Maybe L. Stone is some geeky thirteen-year-old boy."

"So?" Ian jerked his hand out of her grasp and started to type again. "At least he can hold an intelligent conversation."

Nobody had ever insulted Victoria so thoroughly. She stood behind Ian, unnoticed, contemplating murder. In spite of what she had said, she was certain L. Stone was a girl. It was obvious, wasn't it? Only some glasses-wearing, history-quoting, bookwormish girl would pick a handle like L. Stone. Watching Ian type love letters to another girl was hardly Victoria's idea of a fun date. She didn't even have a place to sit, and her feet were killing her.

"I'm outta here," Victoria told Ian coldly.

He didn't look away from the screen. "Do you need me to show you out? I don't want to end this conversation with L. Stone. . . ."

"Don't bother," Victoria said. "I think I'm

smart enough to find the front door on my own."

"Okay." Ian was completely uninterested. "Later."

Victoria felt like making a scene. Temper tantrums—screaming, slamming doors—were one of her specialties. *That* would get Ian's attention. Or would it? Victoria could probably smash in Ian's bedroom wall and still not get him to take his eyes off that screen. She decided not to bother. It would be too humiliating if he continued to ignore her. She walked quietly across Ian's room and closed the door softly.

As Victoria started down the stairs she heard voices. Someone nearby was having an intense conversation. Victoria saw two people standing just inside the Houghtons' door, embracing.

Victoria eased down one more step so she could see the people's faces. Just as she'd expected, it was Ian's father and Suzanne's mother. Everyone knew they were dating. The two were so intent on each other, they didn't even notice her presence.

"It's not you," Ms. Willis sobbed. "It's me."

How juicy, Victoria thought. Ms. Willis is giving lover boy the old heave-ho.

"But what are you so afraid of?" Mr. Houghton asked gently.

"Of getting hurt," Ms. Willis said, taking a step away from Mr. Houghton.

"So it's not that you don't care about me?"

"No! You're wonderful. It's just that I've been

hurt in the past, and I'm a little gun shy. And I'm worried about Suzanne."

"Then I won't accept this," Mr. Houghton said firmly. "If you have a problem, I want to help you work it out. We can get through it together."

"I don't know. . . ."

"Listen," Mr. Houghton said. "I know we've only known each other for a short time. But I haven't felt so strongly about a woman since my wife died five years ago. I'm not going to let you scare me away. Whatever it is, I can handle it. I want to help."

Victoria was hooked. She pressed herself against the wall, hardly daring to breathe.

"Swear you won't say anything," Ms. Willis pleaded.

"Of course. You can trust me," Mr. Houghton replied.

Ms. Willis took a deep breath. "I told my daughter a terrible lie," she said. "And now I'm afraid she's going to find out."

"What kind of lie?" Mr. Houghton asked.

"Suzanne thinks her father is dead," Ms. Willis said. "That's what I've always told her."

"He isn't dead?"

"No," Ms. Willis said. "I just made that up because I was so ashamed—and angry. See, I met him when I was barely older than Suzanne is now. I thought we were in love. Well, I *know* I was. Before I could catch my breath, I was pregnant and he was gone. . . ." Her voice trailed off, and Victoria guessed she had started to cry.

"It's okay," Mr. Houghton said, pulling her closer to him. "It's okay."

"Please," Ms. Willis pleaded. "Please don't tell anyone."

"I won't," Mr. Houghton promised. "Your secret is safe with me. And I don't think it's so terrible. You just wanted to protect Suzanne, didn't you?"

Victoria couldn't hear Ms. Willis's muffled reply.

"Come on," Mr. Houghton said. "Let's get you some tissues and a glass of wine. Everything is going to be okay."

Mr. Houghton led Ms. Willis farther into the house. Victoria waited until she thought they were safely out of sight, then she tiptoed down the stairs. As she passed the living room she could see the adults locked in a passionate embrace. She quietly let herself out the door, certain they hadn't detected her presence.

Victoria hurried to her car and quickly drove away. She was almost glad her date with Ian had been so awful. If it had gone well, she wouldn't have been leaving so early—and she wouldn't have heard what had to be the biggest secret in all of Hillcrest. Her plans for Suzanne Willis's future were already taking shape.

About the Author

Jennifer Baker is the author of two dozen young adult and middle grade novels. She is also the producer for TV Guide Online's teen area and teaches creative writing workshops for elementary and junior high school students. She lives in New York City with her husband and son.

Printed in the United States
By Bookmasters